Spark OF Magic

TRISTA ANN MICHAELS

ELLORA'S CAVE
ROMANTICA PUBLISHING

What the critics are saying…

ร๑

5 Hearts "SPARK OF MAGIC is a humorous, action-packed, sexy romance with two times the punch of most normal romances! […] The plot is fun, fast-paced and well able to keep your interest. It contains just enough surprises to keep you guessing until the end. The sex scenes are fantastic and include ménage, biting and the normal rounds of oral and anal play. I really enjoyed SPARK OF MAGIC and will definitely check out more of Ms. Michaels work as this was a fun and engaging read!" ~ *Dark Angel Reviews*

3/4 Rating "Ms. Michaels leads her reader on a wild magical ride in *Spark of Magic*. I found myself laughing until I cried every time the boy's uncle Vincent strolls in to steal the scene. […] There are so many plot twist sand interesting characters that it was hard to put down once I started." ~ *Just Erotic Romance Reviews*

An Ellora's Cave Romantica Publication

www.ellorascave.com

Spark of Magic

ISBN 9781419958977
ALL RIGHTS RESERVED.
Spark of Magic Copyright © 2008 Trista Ann Michaels
Edited by Ann Leveille.
Photography and cover art by Les Byerley.

This book printed in the U.S.A. by Jasmine-Jade Enterprises
LLC.

Electronic book Publication July 2008
Trade paperback Publication February 2009

This book is a work of fiction and any resemblance to persons
living or dead, or places, events or locales is purely
coincidental. The characters are productions of the author's
imagination and used fictitiously.

SPARK OF MAGIC

ॐ

Trademarks Acknowledgement

The author acknowledges the trademarked status and trademark owners of the following wordmarks mentioned in this work of fiction:

Bewitched: Screen Gems, Inc.

Fantasy Island: Columbia Pictures Industries, Inc.

Harry Potter: Warner Bros. Entertainment, Inc.

Jacuzzi: Jacuzzi Inc.

LoJack: LoJack Corporation

Chapter One

∽

"I can't do this anymore."

Rebecca slammed her apartment door behind her and glared at her best friend Tonya, who glanced up from her magazine with a frown.

"It went that bad?"

"Worse than bad," she said then dropped onto the couch, sinking into the soft suede cushions. "Tell me the truth, Tonya. Is there a sign on my forehead that reads 'losers welcome'?"

Tonya giggled softly and set her magazine aside. "Didn't he have any redeeming qualities? At least one? He was gorgeous."

Rebecca sighed. "Gorgeous does not mean gentleman or even smart. All he talked about was himself and his money. And, of course, let's not forget his little trick of slipping a drug into my drink."

Tonya gasped and sat forward, her green eyes widening in shock. "He did *what?*"

"You know that mirror that hangs behind the bar at the Pinnacle Room?" Tonya nodded and Rebecca continued, "I was at the bar and happened to look up into that mirror and see him slip a small blue pill into my drink and then stir it. I guess he didn't feel confident enough to get me into bed on his own, he felt he had to drug me."

"Oh God," Tonya sighed and dropped her head in her hand. "What did you do?"

Rebecca pursed her lips, trying to stop the blush that quickly moved up her neck. Tonya glanced up at her and scowled. "Rebecca?"

"All right," she sighed, and dropped her head back to stare at the ceiling. "I just did a little something." She held her forefinger and thumb close together. "The waiter just happened to be walking by and he tripped, spilling hot coffee all over my date's crotch." She winced then studied her nails. "Tragic, tragic accident."

"Accident my ass," Tonya said with a grin. "With those powers of yours I'd hate to be your enemy."

Rebecca pouted at her friend of fifteen years. "I never said I used my powers."

Tonya raised an eyebrow. "So the waiter just tripped? With no help from you?"

"Well," Rebecca sighed. "Maybe he had a *little* help from me."

Tonya put her hand over her mouth to hide her giggle then sobered when Rebecca didn't join her in laughter. "Oh, honey. I'm so sorry."

Rebecca remained silent, staring solemnly at the ceiling. This always happened to her. Every guy she'd ever been out with had turned into a jerk. Just last week she'd gone out with someone who'd tried to have sex with her in the damn parking lot of the restaurant. She just didn't understand it.

Tears gathered in her eyes and she tried to swallow the lump that had formed in her throat. Fatigue weighed her down, made her feel depressed. Would the right guy ever come along? And just who was the right guy? Unfortunately she hadn't met just one guy who could do it for her. Usually it took two men to really get her going.

The first time it had happened, she'd gone to a bar with Tonya and had a little too much to drink, letting her inhibitions free. Two guys began flirting with her and the next thing she knew they were at a dark corner table fondling each other like they were starving for one another. Lust had screamed through her that night with the force of a tidal wave.

Her panties had been soaked, her nipples hard and engorged. Just thinking about it now made her wet.

For a long time she'd wondered if something was wrong with her—if she was weird. Eventually she accepted her little quirk. Fantasizing about two men was only one of her many little oddities. The other was her ability to do magic with the flick her hand.

She'd first discovered her talent at the age of fifteen. Tonya had been the only one she told. Her friend was the only one she trusted for she was an orphan, like her. It wasn't like she had anyone else. Her foster parents certainly hadn't been interested. She had no idea who her real parents were and honestly, she wasn't sure she cared.

She and Tonya had spent months researching her powers, reading everything about witches and witchcraft, extra sensory perception and anything else that might explain her abilities. They finally determined she was what they called a "natural witch". She could make things happen without the use of spells. Tonya thought it was an amazing gift but to Rebecca it was a curse. Too bad her powers couldn't help her find what she needed. Too bad they couldn't give her the answers she'd tried so hard to find.

"Rebecca?"

As a single tear slipped down Rebecca's cheek she turned her head to stare at her friend. "What's wrong with me, Tonya? Why can't I find the right guy?"

"I don't know, honey. But he's out there, I know it."

"I wish you were right but I'm beginning to think he—or they—don't exist." With a loud sigh she turned back to the ceiling. "I need a good lay. A really good one, you know? I need something my vibrator and anal wand can't give me."

Tonya snorted. "What you need is to have your head examined. I can't believe you really want to have sex with two men. You just think you do. If you could find the right guy, you wouldn't need two men. You would just need him."

"I don't know," she whispered then rose to her feet. "I'm going to go take a hot bath, wallow in self-pity for a while then go to bed."

"Are you sure you should be alone?"

"Yeah. I'll be fine."

Rebecca waved then headed to the privacy of her bathroom and her huge Jacuzzi tub.

* * * * *

"Tell me you saw that."

"I think everyone saw it," Nicholas chuckled then glanced at his twin brother, Darien, across from him. "I'd hate to be that guy. A scalded cock can't be pleasant."

The restaurant had settled down, the commotion was over and the young female witch gone. But they knew how to find her. Her powers would lead them right to her door. Now that they'd seen her use them they would be like a beacon pointing the way.

"Not the imbecile. He had it coming. The girl."

"Yes, I saw it." Nicholas smiled. "She's still young, still not in full control of her powers."

"I agree. She waved her hand. Apparently she doesn't know yet that's not needed. How will we manage it?" Darien asked, his brow creasing in a frown. "There's only one way to know if she's the one."

Nicholas nodded. He certainly wanted her to be the one. The second he'd seen her standing at the bar, her sable hair cascading down her back, he couldn't seem to look away. She was beautiful and made his breath catch. He couldn't remember the last time a woman had made his heart jerk with just a look.

He'd kept watching her, knew the second she'd realized what her date had done. He'd seen her expression darken in the mirror behind the bar and her lips thin. Her deep emerald green eyes had sparked fire and his cock had jerked at the intensity he saw in their depths.

He and his brother had searched unsuccessfully for years for the child of Korinda and Shane. Their father had made them promise just before his death to find her, to keep the daughter of his best friend safe from Sebastian's clutches. This could be her, she had eyes like Korinda's, but the only true way to tell would be to join with her.

"We should get her to the club," Nicholas said thoughtfully. "See which fantasy she chooses."

Darien smiled. "I'll take care of it."

"Do it discreetly. We don't want Sebastian catching wind of her. Not yet."

* * * * *

Rebecca shifted the bags in her hand and smiled as a breeze blew, ruffling her hair and cooling her heated skin. Downtown Boston was gorgeous and filled with shops and restaurants but all the concrete elevated the already sweltering temperatures.

"I love that top you got," Tonya said, pulling Rebecca's mind from the weather.

Rebecca grinned. "You're just saying that because you want to borrow it."

"Well of course. That's what I keep you around for after all. You have great taste in clothes."

With a laugh Rebecca pointed to a small bench. "Let's sit down for a minute."

Rebecca dropped onto the bench, sighing as she studied her tired feet strapped into the three-inch heels. "I knew I shouldn't have worn these shoes."

"Yeah, but they look great."

Rebecca snorted. "A lot of good it does me if I can't walk."

"Are you feeling better? I know you were pretty upset last night."

Sitting back against the bench, she adjusted the bags next to her to avoid looking at her friend. She really wasn't better but didn't want to worry Tonya.

"I think, but I had a really weird dream last night."

"What kind of dream?" Tonya asked.

Squinting, Rebecca tried to remember. "There were these two guys. I couldn't really see their faces but could tell they had long, black hair and I knew instinctively they were identical." She also knew instinctively she belonged with them. That they were her path to happiness and understanding who she was.

"What happened?"

Rebecca glanced at her friend in surprise. She hadn't realized she'd been quiet, her mind on the men. "It started out very sexy. Two men being very passionate…gentle. But then it changed and I was being chased by another man. A man I knew wanted to hurt me. He was evil." She shivered as the distorted images ran through her mind.

Tonya smiled. "I think you've been watching too many scary movies."

Rebecca laughed as well. "Maybe you're right."

"You need to relax, Becca. You've been under a lot of stress lately. This isn't the first bad dream you've had. You're distracted, uptight."

"I know," she sighed. "I'm not sure what's wrong with me. I just feel like something's missing."

"Like what?"

"I don't know if it's anything specific or even material. It's almost like I'm in the wrong place?" She turned to look at her friend. "Like…there's something I need to be doing."

Tonya reached out and patted her knee. "You'll figure it out, I know you will."

Something nudged at her leg and she glanced down, surprised to see a small black dog staring at her and wagging its tail. "Oh my God," she laughed, bending to ruffle the small dog's ear. "Where did you come from?"

"Is that a Maltese?" Tonya asked. "Those are expensive dogs. Does it have a tag?"

Rebecca felt around the dog's neck. She shook her head. "I don't feel one. Are you all alone?"

The dog lifted onto its back feet and licked at Rebecca's face, making her laugh. "Oh, you're so cute. Should we take it home with us?"

"Surely it belongs to someone."

Sitting up, Rebecca glanced around the street. No one seemed to be looking for him. Was he lost? The dog stuck his head in her purse and she smiled, tugging at the straps to get it away from him. "What are you doing?" asked with a giggle then gasped when the dog removed his head, her key chain dangling from his mouth.

With an almost mischievous look the dog took off down the street.

"Oh my God!" Rebecca exclaimed. "The little devil has my keys."

Grabbing their bags, they both took off after the dog. He stayed well ahead of them, his small body maneuvering through the crowd easily.

"Rebecca, wait. You can open locks with magic, you don't really need those keys."

Rebecca stopped running and took a deep breath. "It has my work keys on it. If I ever quit my job I would need to return them. Besides, I don't want to rely on magic for everything. I want to be normal, Tonya."

Tonya nodded and pointed toward the dog, which had stopped and was now watching them with interest. "Check it out. I think the little mongrel is playing with us."

"This is insane."

"Can you use magic to stop him?"

Rebecca shook her head. "I don't know."

The Maltese took a couple of steps forward, watching them closely. Taking a deep breath, Rebecca tried to concentrate on holding the dog still, until he snorted.

"Did that little dog just snort?" Tonya asked, trying to stifle a giggle.

Rebecca frowned. She had to get those keys. Handing Tonya her two bags, she took off after him again, having to jog to keep up with his little legs. She loved dogs, especially little ones. But this dog... His game of keep away was beginning to grate on her last nerve. She needed those keys.

He turned a corner and Rebecca followed, Tonya close behind her. She scanned the streets, her heart skipping when she didn't immediately see him. "Do you see him?" she asked Tonya.

"There."

Rebecca looked to where Tonya pointed and saw the little bugger run into a building. Both girls took off as well. The doors were open and without looking at what type of business they were headed into they barreled through the opening, only to stop and stare wide-eyed at the darkened interior.

Numerous tables surrounded a crowded, circular bar. The room was dark with black walls and red tablecloths. Candles flickered everywhere, flooding the room with soft light. Candelabras hung from the ceiling, thick off-white candles dripping wax onto the wrought iron holding them and giving the room a gothic appearance.

People turned to look at them in surprise and the heat of a blush moved over Rebecca's face.

"Ladies, may I help you?"

They both turned to face the man who'd spoken. Probably the manager ready to chew them out for barreling into his bar like they had. He was tall and muscular with intense eyes and short black hair. Quite a hunk and Rebecca didn't miss the way Tonya's fingers dug into her elbow.

"Oh my," Tonya murmured.

* * * * *

Nicholas dropped the keys onto the floor and morphed back into his human form. He worked his tired jaw, ignoring his brother's amused chuckle. "You couldn't think of anything better than a Maltese?" Darien asked with amusement.

He snorted. "Somehow I don't think a Doberman would have gotten the same attention." Bending, he picked the keys from the floor.

Darien sat straighter. "So she followed you?"

"Yes. Ready to make ourselves known? See what her reaction is?"

With a nod, Darien followed him from the storage room and out into the main area of their club. The upper level was a restaurant, the lower level a hedonistic area catering to sexual fantasies—an area they hoped to lure Rebecca to for the night. If she was the one they were looking for, when they joined they would know. And so would Sebastian. They had to tread carefully.

Walking out into the main room, Nicholas found her immediately. She looked beautiful in white slacks and a pink top, her long blonde hair pulled back in a loose ponytail at her nape, small gold hoop earrings dangling from her ears. Delicate and dainty was how he would describe the vision standing a few feet away. His heart thumped wildly just looking at her.

As the dog, he could smell her scent very well and it still lingered in the air around him, settling around his heart like a blanket of warmth. God help him if this wasn't the woman they needed to find. Shifting her keys in his hand, he slid his finger through the ring and held them up, jingling them to get her attention.

"These must belong to you."

Rebecca stared wide-eyed at the man who'd just spoken, her car keys dangling from his fingers. He was tall, with long black hair cascading around wide shoulders and eyes the most intense shade of deep blue she'd ever seen stared back at her, watching carefully. Behind him stood a man identical to the one who'd spoken, also watching with just a hint of amusement glittering in his gaze.

Her breath caught in her throat, leaving her unable to speak. Something about them seemed familiar and smacked of déjà vu. Images from her dream ran across her mind. It wasn't anything physical, more like an emotional tug pulling her toward them like a beacon.

Tonya nudged her and she cleared her throat quickly. "Yes, I'm sorry. Those are mine. Thank you."

She reached out to take them but he pulled them back, just slightly out of her reach. Her gaze caught his and he smiled, making her stomach tighten. "I'd like to apologize for the dog. He finds stuff like this amusing."

Her eye brow rose in skepticism. "The *dog* finds it amusing?" *More like the owner does.*

"Yes. You'd be surprised at just how human that dog is."

Glancing over his shoulder, she noticed his twin's lips twitch.

"I'm Nicholas, by the way." Her gaze shot back to his and he nodded behind him. "And this is my brother, Darien. We own this place and as repayment for the trouble our dog caused I'd like for Marcus here to give you a tour of the club. Anything you want to do or experience is on us."

Tonya again nudged her and she glanced at her friend, who gazed pointedly at Marcus. Rebecca knew what she wanted. With a sigh she relented, although secretly she'd hoped the twins would stick around, maybe join them in their explorations. Something about them made her feel all dreamy. It was nuts, wasn't it, to have that kind of reaction to men at first sight?

"I'll hold on to your keys until you're ready to go," Nicholas said, his eyes sparkling and making her stomach flutter. "It will guarantee I'll see you again."

Chapter Two

ᦆ

Marcus led them to a set of double doors at the back of the room with a wink toward Tonya. Rebecca frowned as she tried to recall the outside layout of the building. It hadn't appeared to be all that big but then she had been chasing a dog at the time. The second the doors opened, revealing a wide staircase leading to a basement, her confusion disappeared.

"I know where we are. I can't believe I didn't notice when we first ran in here," Tonya murmured close to her ear.

"Where?"

"Dreamshire."

Rebecca gulped. "The hedonistic club?"

She heard of it but never imagined this is what it would look like. She'd considered it once or twice, to try her ménage fantasy on for size, see if it fit. But the club had been too expensive for her. She turned to look over her shoulder and noticed one of the twins watching her. He raised his glass of wine in salute and she smiled slightly before turning her attention back to the stairs.

"Can you believe our luck?" Tonya whispered in her ear. "And would you check out our escort? Now there's a man I wouldn't mind fulfilling my fantasies with." Her gaze admired their escort's firm backside. "He's gorgeous."

Rebecca smiled at her friend's obvious infatuation and gently nudged her. "Don't you think you should shop a little?"

Tonya snorted, making Rebecca giggle. Marcus smiled at them over his shoulder and she got the distinct impression he knew they were talking about him.

"It's the middle of the day," he began. "So there're not many people here. Things will pick up on the weekend."

Warm air lifted from the level below them, ruffling Rebecca's bangs. Taking deep breaths for courage, they slowly descended the stairs to the basement. Tonya's fingers tightened on her arm and Rebecca stole a sideways glance toward her friend. Her face was aglow with excitement, her eyes wide with an almost childlike glee. Rebecca wished she could feel that same excitement. Instead she felt nervous, apprehensive—as though something more than just a fantasy awaited her in the bowls of this club.

"But you're free to choose any fantasy you might like," Marcus added.

He smiled at Tonya and Rebecca suddenly felt like a third wheel. The attraction between the two of them was obvious.

As they descended the final steps into the massive room Rebecca couldn't help but stare in awe. Around them were scenarios, each roped off, depicting sexual fantasies. The figures were made of wax but their facial expressions were depicted with a clarity that was almost unreal. Eyes sparkled with lust, a sheen of sweat covered their brows, their chests. She almost expected to see one of them move, inhaling a gulp of air.

Tonya dragged her toward the flogging fantasy. A woman stood tied between two posts, her hands held high above her head, her lips open in a silent scream. The flogger had left light red welts along her flesh. Her nipples were erect, the skin of her inner thighs wet. A man stood to her side, his hand raised to swing the flogger toward her hips. His face was obscured. Only his blue, piercing eyes shone through the slits of his mask. The attention to detail was utterly amazing.

His chest was bare, his arms thick and muscular, a pair of leather pants hugged his hips and thighs. It was quite an erotic image and she had to admit it turned her on. Even if she only admitted it to herself.

"Please explore at your leisure, ladies," their escort said and Rebecca turned to stare at him in surprise. She'd forgotten he was there.

"Is this it? We just walk around the room and stare at the various fantasies played out in wax?"

"Of course not, unless of course that's your fantasy," he said with a grin. "Once you pick your fantasy you step past the ropes."

"Step past the ropes?" she and Tonya asked in surprise.

He nodded then walked forward, slipping his hand past the rope and into the scene. His hand began to slowly disappear as he moved forward. They both gasped and stepped back, watching in shock as the scene seemed to swallow him.

Rebecca shook her head in denial, her eyes glued to the man's arm, now disappearing up to his elbow. She slowly began to relax as ideas of how it worked came to her. "Is it mirrors?" she asked. "Or some kind of holographic wall?"

Their escort pulled his arm free and smiled. "No. It's magic."

"Magic?" Rebecca asked skeptically.

Tonya snorted. "You of all people, Becca, should know what magic is."

Rebecca ignored her friend and stepped forward, examining the scene more closely. "So you're saying if we find a fantasy we want to experience we just step through that invisible wall and we're inside it." She pointed toward the woman tied up. "I would be her? I would take her place within the scene?"

"Yes."

"What about the man?" Tonya asked. "Is he experiencing a fantasy as well or is he part of the club?"

"If there is a man who wishes to be in the fantasy, then it's that man. If not then it will be an employee from the club.

W e have numerous safety measures in place so you never have to worry about being hurt, unless of course that is your fantasy and even those are watched closely."

"Amazing," Tonya said as she slowly moved about the room, checking out the different fantasies. With a grin she glanced at Rebecca from the corner of her eye. "Wonder how you apply for that job?"

A spark of light in the dark room caught Rebecca's attention and she turned just in time to see a woman emerge from the sex in public fantasy. Behind her a crowd of wax figures gathered around a woman greedily licking a thick cock. The people around her smiled and looked as though they were cheering her on. The man's wax hand gripped the base, holding it at her lips while his other hand held her head steady.

The woman leaving the fantasy wiped her lips with a satisfied smile then turned to stare at Rebecca in surprise. "Oh, hello. Here to find a fantasy?"

Rebecca shrugged. "I guess so. Is it really like that?" she asked, pointing toward the wax reenactment.

The woman looked over her shoulder at the scene and grinned. "With amazing accuracy." She nodded her head toward the scene depicting sex in a hot tub, a snowy mountain behind them, steam slowly rising to surround the participants. "That's where I'm headed next."

With a wink, she took off toward the scene then practically jumped through the invisible wall, disappearing inside the fantasy. Tonya came to stand next to Rebecca, her eyes wide with shock. "This is crazy," she whispered.

Rebecca nodded then looked at their escort. He stood to the side, patiently waiting for them to make their choice. "Now that she's in there, does that mean the fantasy is taken?" Tonya asked.

"No. You may enter as well. When you do it becomes your fantasy just as it became hers when she stepped through."

"I think I may try that one," Tonya mused and Rebecca's lips spread into a slight grin.

"Not something more wild? Just that?"

"What do you mean just that?" Tonya said with a snort. "Do you have any idea how long it's been since I've had good sex? I don't want anything frilly. I just want good sex."

Rebecca chuckled. "Yeah, I know what you mean."

"No you don't," Tonya teased. "You want frilly. Do you have any ménage à trois fantasies?" Tonya asked their escort and Rebecca rolled her eyes.

"Of course," he said with a nod. "Those are on the far wall."

Tonya grabbed her hand and tugged her toward the scenes. Rebecca's heart raced wildly as she studied the scenarios before her. There were three, one a BDSM scene with the woman tied up. She grimaced and shook her head at Tonya. Her friend grinned then pulled her toward the next one.

The middle image depicted three men and one woman. Although erotic, it wasn't quite what she had in mind. Raising an eyebrow at Tonya, her friend shrugged then pulled her along to the third fantasy.

This one was intriguing. A woman sat on her knees, bent slightly forward as she licked at a man's cock in front of her. Another man behind her fucked her pussy with two fingers. Rebecca could feel her own pussy getting wet as she stared at the erotic image. She swallowed a sudden strong wave of lust that had her almost jumping through the wall. In her mind she imagined the two men as Nicholas and Darien. With a blink, she tried to shove the image away. Why would they be down here, or with her for that matter?

"You know you want to," Tonya purred in her ear and she jerked in surprise.

"You cannot lie with your fantasies," their escort murmured.

"What do you mean?" Rebecca whispered, her gaze glued to the image.

"It means the fantasy knows. It knows your heart and will transform to meet your true fantasy."

"So you mean no matter which fantasy she goes into it will change to what she really wants?" Tonya asked.

"To a certain degree, yes. If she'd chosen the sex in public fantasy it would still be sex in public but there would be two men instead of just one if that is what she truly desires."

"Interesting," Tonya mused. "Give it a shot, honey. Go in."

Rebecca licked her lips as she stared at the cock settled before the woman's lips. It was so thick and long. Would whoever was in there be as big? Would they be good? Would it be what she needed?

With a gentle nudge between her shoulder blades, Tonya pushed her toward the wall. *Here goes nothing.* Taking a deep breath, she stepped through and into the fantasy.

* * * * *

Darien and Nicholas stood off to the side and watched with excitement as Rebecca stepped through. "She went in," Darien said, his body already aching to be close to her heat. He could already feel her tug and he had no doubt she was the one they'd been searching for.

"I see that," Nicholas said. "And she even chose the ménage."

Darien smiled as he imagined her lips wrapped around his cock, which had already become hard as a damn rock. It wasn't just a physical attraction. He'd had plenty of that.

When he looked at Rebecca there was an emotional tug, a feeling of belonging he'd never felt before. Every time he looked at her he thought of forever. "Shall we join her?" he murmured.

"I thought you'd never ask," Nicholas replied and with a wink they were transported into the fantasy.

* * * * *

Tonya watched Rebecca go with a grin then turned to study several of the other fantasies around her. Her gaze kept wandering to the escort who still followed close behind. He watched her with a deep blue gaze that sent her heart racing, like a hungry wolf determined to devour his prey. Handsome wasn't quite the word she would use to describe him. He was beautiful—dangerous, sultry, steamy… She smiled. Wicked.

He had short, deep black hair that topped a rugged face and wide shoulders. As her gaze wandered downward she wondered what his chest looked like beneath that shirt. Was his it sprinkled with hair or was it smooth and tan, stretched tight over hard, bulging muscles?

Her pussy clenched and she rolled her eyes, turning away from the gorgeous escort. She was supposed to be picking out a fantasy, not fantasizing about her quiet host. But there was something about him. She couldn't stop looking at him, couldn't stop thinking about his arms around her.

Like Rebecca, all she really wanted was a man to take care of her, love her, cherish her. Licking her lips, she glanced back at his eyes and felt a warmth surround her—a feeling of belonging. Was she out of her mind or had she just been without sex too long?

"Have you ever done one of these?" she asked, watching him from the corner of her eye.

"Yes," he answered.

"Which one?" With a grin, she pointed toward the flogging scene they'd studied earlier. "That one?"

She could see him as a dominant. She could even see herself as his submissive. Now wouldn't that be fun?

He remained silent, his lips spreading into a slow sensual smile that made her heart skip a beat.

"I bet you've done them all, haven't you?" she teased, not truly believing what she was doing. Flirting with her host? Shouldn't she be jumping into one of these fantasies instead of lusting after the one guy she probably couldn't have right now? He was working, after all.

"Yes," he said with another grin.

"What was your favorite?"

"The one with you."

Her grin faded and she stared at him, stunned. "I beg your pardon?"

He walked closer, his hand rising to touch the small device in his ear. "Hey, Shawn. Cover for me in the fantasy room."

Tonya couldn't hear what was said on the other end but she had a feeling Shawn had agreed because Marcus pulled the device out of his ear, letting it hang around his neck.

Tonya's heart hammered in excitement as he loomed over her, his blue eyes shining with the same lust gripping her. "My favorite is whichever fantasy you want, Tonya," he repeated.

"You know my name?"

He grinned. "I heard your friend call you that."

"Oh," she mouthed, frowning and trying to remember. Had Rebecca called her by name?

His eyes raked over her body, sending tingles of prickly heat down her spine. God he was gorgeous.

"Pick one and I'll follow you in," he murmured, his eyes dancing mischievously.

"You can do that?" she gasped, her pussy already drenched and hungry.

"I can do anything I want."

Her lips twitched in amusement and excitement as he wrapped his arm around her lower back and pulled her close.

"I don't know," she murmured, placing her hands at his waist. The material of his black turtleneck did nothing to hide the twitching of his muscles. "Sex with a complete stranger? Will you still respect me tomorrow?" she teased.

Marcus laughed. A deep laugh that rumbled through his whole body and sent tingles down her spine. "Of course I will," he murmured against her lips. "Hurry up and pick a fantasy, sweet, before I fuck you right here."

Her heart skipped a beat as she stared deep into his gaze. This was crazy, wasn't it? Nuts? She'd never in her life done this—seduced a man she didn't even know—but for some reason it felt so right—like if she didn't do this she'd be losing the best thing to ever happen to her.

"Maybe that's my fantasy," she whispered. "Maybe I want you to fuck me right here. Right here on a table in clear view of anyone who might walk in."

Marcus's nostrils flared and his eyes darkened. "That table?" he asked with a nod toward the rectangular wooden table set up in the middle of the room.

She didn't know why she hadn't noticed it before but none of that mattered now. This man was her fantasy. This man, that table and one mind-blowing night of sex she would remember for years to come.

"That table," she murmured, pushing him backward.

Marcus grinned and put his hands on her ass, lifting her easily to wrap her legs around his waist. Her pussy rested against the ridge of his shaft and she wiggled, rubbing herself along the length of his hard cock. Oh god he was huge and juices poured from her pussy as she imagined how good he'd feel inside her.

His fingers bunched her skirt up around her waist, leaving her hips and pussy exposed.

"Fuck," Marcus growled, setting her on the edge of the table.

The wood was cold against her ass but she barely noticed, instead focusing on Marcus as he spread her thighs, his gaze feasting on her wet pussy. She hadn't worn underwear and at the moment she was counting her lucky stars. Her body burned everywhere for his touch.

"Nice and wet," he whispered.

"It's all these images," she whispered as his fingers slowly drew through her juices, separating her swollen labia.

"Are you sure that's all it is?" he whispered, placing a kiss on the smooth flesh just above her clit. "Maybe I was your fantasy all along."

His tongue flicked across her clit and she gasped, bucking her hips toward his mouth. "Oh God," she groaned and bit down on her lower lip. "Maybe you were. You certainly do that like in my fantasies."

His lips spread into a naughty grin before he licked along her slit, lapping at the juices pouring from her channel.

"Such a sweet pussy," he murmured before thrusting his tongue deep inside her passage.

She gasped, falling back to lie on the table, her legs thrown over his shoulders as he licked his fill. Her hips bucked and ground, searching out a firmer touch she knew would send her soaring. It had been so long since she'd had an orgasm—so long since she'd been with anyone who could make her feel like this.

"Marcus," she moaned as his tongue slowly circled her sensitive nub.

Two fingers thrust into her channel, making her hips buck off the table and causing her clit to lose contact with Marcus' tongue. She groaned, rolling her head from side to side as he gently fucked her with his fingers. With his other hand he undid his pants, freeing his huge shaft.

She licked her lips in excitement as he settled the head at her pussy. His fingers moved to toy with the tight hole of her anus and her muscles clenched in anticipation. Her whole body shivered at the dark lust centering there. Slowly he slid his cock forward, filling her to the womb. She groaned, lifting her hips to take him deeper. As she did his fingers pressed into her ass, filling her with a burning need demanding to be quenched.

"Ah," he groaned, holding himself still inside her. "Such a hot little pussy you have, sweet. It feels so good."

She ground her hips against him, wanting more, wanting him to pound into her hard. What had gotten into her? Why couldn't she get enough? Why did it feel so perfect?

He groaned, holding her hips still by putting pressure on her lower stomach with his free hand. He pulled out then pressed back in slowly, inch by excruciating inch, his fingers still pressed deep in her ass.

"Like that, sweet?" he murmured then did it again, driving her insane with his patience and slow movements.

He pulled out, circling her swollen clit with the head of his shaft. Lightning zeroed in on the tiny little nub, robbing her of breath. "Answer me," he demanded and her heart jerked. How did he know she liked being ordered, being dominated? "Answer me or I won't give you what you want."

He kept teasing her, kept toying with her clit.

"Yes I like it," she sighed and he thrust slowly back inside her, wringing a scream from deep inside her chest. "Oh yes, I like it. Harder, Marcus. Give it to me harder."

"In time," he cooed then removed his fingers from her ass to slap her hip.

She gasped, the sting sending shards of pleasure to her already screaming core. All it would take would be one hard, deep thrust to send her over the edge and she had a feeling he knew it. Like her, he wanted to keep it slow, savor the feel of it.

"Undo your top," he ordered, keeping his thrusts shallow and slow. "Let me see your pretty breasts."

With trembling fingers she tugged her top open. She pulled at the lace covering her breasts, freeing them to spill over the top of her bra. The cool air of the room blew across her nipples, hardening them, sensitizing them. Leaning forward, Marcus licked at the tip of her breasts, making juices pour from her pussy to coat the table and his cock. His thrusts remained shallow, slow, as he licked his fill of one breast and then the other.

She tried to undulate her hips, tried to take him deeper, but he kept her still. When her orgasm came it would be mind-blowing, she knew it deep inside. Her muscles were already tensing and pulsing, sucking at his cock hungrily.

"That feels so good," he murmured as he stood straight and thrust deep but not deep enough for the base of his cock to hit her clit. She moaned, slapping her hands against the table, desperate now for release. Any relief.

"I like how your pussy sucks at my cock, sweet. I like how it feels as it tightens around me."

Tonya sighed in answer, lifting her hips and matching his slow rhythm. "Want it harder, sweet?" he purred, pulling almost out.

"Yes," she hissed then cried out when he slammed into her hard, scooting her across the table.

Gripping her hips, he held her still as he continued to pummel her, his balls slapping against her ass in a pounding rhythm that sent her soaring out of control. Every nerve ending in her body screamed with release and pleasure as her pussy gripped his cock, holding tight as she rode out the waves of her orgasm.

Marcus groaned along with her, his head thrown back as a strangled cry left his throat to mingle with her own sighs of pleasure.

Chapter Three

80

Rebecca stared in awe at the tropical surroundings. A path in front of her led to a secluded beach. The full moon cast silvery light across the waves and the warm night breeze blew across her shoulders like a caress as she stepped through the brush and onto the white sands of the beach.

Everything was amazing and so realistic, right down to the soft sounds of the waves crashing against the shore and the scent of tropical flowers floating on the breeze. *How did they do that?* she wondered as she strolled closer to the water. Even her clothes had changed. With a frown, she glanced down at her two-piece bathing suit. Moonlight twinkled against her silver belly button ring and she brushed her finger around it before raising her gaze to stare out at the water.

Where were her men? Where were the men who were supposed to help bring this fantasy to life?

"Beautiful night, isn't it?"

She gasped and turned to stare in surprise at the twins from earlier. They were shirtless, their bronze skin stretched tight over bulging muscles. Every inch of them glowed golden in the moonlight and her fingers itched to touch their flesh, see if it was as smooth as it appeared to be. As her gaze traveled downward she realized they were naked, their cocks jutting outward, ready to give her all she imagined she wanted.

Was this for real? Was it really them or had this...this room conjured them up from her mind because she'd seen them earlier? They were the owners, the very men who'd held her keys upstairs.

"We're quite real," the closest one said as though reading her mind. She frowned as she studied him more closely.

32

"Which one are you?" she asked, finally deciding to just run with the fantasy. To hell with the real world.

"Nicholas," he whispered.

Both of them strolled closer, their bodies moving with amazing catlike grace. Her heart hammered wildly in her chest but the idea of moving never entered her mind. It was though some force held her immobile. She trusted them and for the life of her she didn't understand why.

"I'm Rebecca," she whispered, unsure what else to say.

"We know," Darien murmured in her ear and a sliver of heat traveled down her spine. "We met earlier, remember?"

She nodded, inhaling their musky scents. "Are you really here? Or did my mind just put you here?"

"We're very real, Rebecca," Darien whispered.

His fingers moved slowly beneath the straps of her top, pulling them down as he trailed a blazing path down her arms with the pads of his fingers. She stared, entranced, into Nicholas' gaze, unable to look away as Darien unclasped the back of her top, letting it fall forgotten to the sand at her feet. The night breeze washed across her nipples, making them harden and ache. Her breasts were full and needed so desperately to be squeezed and licked.

Darien cupped them from behind and she dropped her head back with a moan. His hands were warm and soft but firm as he kneaded her mounds. Lifting one, he offered it to Nicholas, who leaned down and licked her engorged nipple.

Rebecca sighed, arching her back to better fit her breasts into Nicholas' face. But Nicholas took his time, gently stroking around the nipple with his tongue before engulfing the tip into his hot mouth and sucking hard. Rebecca let out a rasping cry, lifting her hands to bury them in his soft hair and tug him closer. His teeth scraped across her nipple, making her shudder in need.

She forgot all her concerns and let her inhibitions run wild. It was like being in a dream. A perfect dream. Juices coated her pussy and the crotch of her bathing suit as Darien gently nibbled along the side of her neck, his teeth softly biting at her pulse point. Every muscle in her body felt weak and mushy, her insides like molten lava, ready to be taken any way they chose.

Oh yes, this fantasy fit. It fit so well and felt so right.

"Can you feel it, Nicholas?" Darien questioned.

Nicholas removed his mouth from her breast and dropped to his knees before her so he could tug at the bottoms of her suit. "Yes," he hissed, leaning in closer to inhale her scent.

Feel what, she wondered, but their hands quickly made her forget.

Nicholas' palms pushed her bottom of her bathing suit to the ground then helped her to lift shaking legs and step out of them. With a gentle shove he spread her legs wide, allowing him access to her aching core. Two fingers gently spread her juices along her slit then upward between her ass cheeks.

She trembled from head to toe, falling back onto Darien's chest. He caught her easily, holding her with one arm around her waist, the other fondling her breasts. Was it the heat? Is that what Darien had meant when he'd asked Nicholas if he felt it? The ever-increasing heat as they came closer to an overwhelming need to find release?

Rebecca couldn't ever remember being so turned-on. She couldn't ever remember being so much in need or so wet. Being with just one man had never been enough for her. She'd always needed two. She'd always needed this.

Nicholas removed his hand to stand before her and she groaned, wanting him to put his hand back, to fuck her with his fingers. Instead he covered her lips with his, filling her mouth with his spicy taste. His tongue was like velvet, stroking hers with wicked intent and she responded in kind, sucking greedily.

Darien's hands stroked down her flesh, igniting her passion to almost boiling. His fingers slid through the juices coating her pussy and her hips jerked backward, seeking a firmer touch. He continued to tease, separating her labia and smearing her juices. Two fingers thrust deep, sending her spiraling upward, her moan becoming lost in Nicholas' kiss.

She could hardly breathe, could hardly think as Darien thrust his fingers in and out, teasing her with the gentle strokes. He removed them, moving to the tight hole of her anus. Gently he pressed forward, testing the ring of resistance before pulling them back and sliding them through the juices coating her pussy.

Rebecca was on fire. Hot, blazing fire that threatened to consume every part of her.

"So beautiful," Nicholas whispered against her lips as his fingers moved down to pinch at her nipples. "So perfect for us."

"So perfect," she murmured. "For me."

"That's it, baby," Darien whispered. "Let us take you, give you what you need."

"Yes," she moaned.

Darien thrust two wet fingers deep into her ass. "Is this where you need it?"

"I need it everywhere," she hissed, pushing her hips back in time with his thrusts.

Nicholas dropped back to his knees and licked his tongue along her slit. She gasped, digging her nails into the flesh of Darien's arm, still wrapped around her waist. His nose nudged her clit, making her gasp, and Darien increased the rhythm of his fingers as they fucked her ass.

"Oh yes," she sighed as Nicholas slid two fingers into her dripping pussy. His movements kept time with Darien's, each pressing against the thin membrane separating her channels, driving her mad with need. She wanted more. She needed more.

"Please, one of you," she gasped.

Nicholas removed his fingers and lay on his back against the sand. Darien removed his as well but instead of letting her sink on Nicholas's delectable cock like she wanted to he told her to drop to her knees.

"Suck his cock," he ordered.

Licking her lips in anticipation she leaned forward, sticking her ass in the air, and drug her tongue along the vein of Nicholas' thick shaft. His cock jerked and she reached out to gently message his balls. Nicholas groaned, holding the back of her head with his palm. Behind her Darien separated the folds of her pussy and stabbed her with his tongue. She groaned, thrusting her hips back in time with his licks as he ate at her juices.

Grasping Nicholas' cock at the base, she lifted it to her lips. Her tongue flicked out to lick at the salty pre-cum coating the head.

"Mmm," Nicholas murmured. "That's it, baby. Lick it like it's your favorite piece of candy."

She continued to stroke him, teasing the tip with her tongue as Darien switched gears and thrust two fingers into her pussy, fucking her hard and fast. She groaned, guiding Nicholas' cock into her mouth and sucking just as furiously. A hunger gripped her unlike anything she'd felt before. She needed to bond with them, needed them slamming her full with their cocks, their strength. Needed it like she needed the air she breathed.

Darien moved closer and replaced his fingers with his thick cock, pressing deep in excruciatingly slow thrusts. She cried out as he stretched her, filled her with his heat.

"Just to get wet," he murmured. "I want your ass, baby. I want to sink my cock into your ass while Nicholas takes your pussy."

Searing heat flared through her body at even the threat of taking both of them at once. It was what she'd spent her whole life waiting for.

"Take me, please," she moaned, almost desperate now.

Darien removed his cock then helped to position her over Nicholas. She sank greedily onto his cock, sighing as he filled her to the womb. With a groan of his own Nicholas tugged her down to his chest as Darien pushed his cock deep into her ass.

At first the sensation overwhelmed her and she fought for air, struggling to remain conscious as the fullness threatened to send her soaring. As she calmed other sensations began to emerge. The feel of her pussy squeezing and sucking at Nicholas' cock, the tightness of her ass around Darien's cock, the belonging that filled all three of them as they began to move as one.

The sensations engulfed her, filled her until she thought she would explode. She didn't know how much more she could take and fought the overwhelming emotions as she wiggled between the two of them, anxious to feel them moving inside her.

"Let it come," Nicholas whispered. "Let it inside you."

"No," she murmured, not completely sure what she was denying. Whatever it was it threatened to consume and it scared the hell out of her.

Slowly they began to move, Darien thrusting in and out as she ground her pussy on Nicholas' hard cock.

"You can't fight it, baby," Darien said as he placed a gentle kiss on her shoulder.

Rebecca whimpered, trying hard to keep that wall up, that one barrier against whatever it was threatening to take her over. Nicholas held her hips still so he could thrust up, deeper into her channel.

"Oh God," she gasped, clinging hard to her control.

Darien thrust harder, keeping tempo with Nicholas and sending her senses to the stratosphere. Tension built in her stomach, knotting her muscles and hardening her breasts. Again sensations nudged at the back of her mind—cocks gripped in hot lava, balls tight and ready to explode. She closed her eyes, fighting the sensations, holding tight to her fear of the unknown. Feeling their pleasure intensified her own but at the same time terrified her.

"Let it in, baby," Nicholas gasped, holding tight to his own control. "Let us in."

They both intensified their thrusts, going deeper, pushing into her harder and wringing every last ounce of control out of her. She screamed as their pleasure came rushing in. Everything they felt, she felt—the tightening of their balls, the slickness of her pussy and the tightness of her ass around Darien's cock. Everything, she felt it all, and when she exploded she not only felt her own world tilting but theirs too as they emptied their seed deep into her body.

With a shout she collapsed onto Nicholas' chest, losing herself in the darkness that followed.

"What the hell just happened?" Darien grunted as he slid his cock out of her tight ass.

Nicholas knew Darien had to be as weak as he was from the multiple orgasms that had gripped them. He'd not only felt his own but Darien's and Rebecca's as well. He'd never imagined it would be that intense and hadn't been prepared for it. He felt as though part of his soul had just been ripped from his chest.

"It would appear that not only is Rebecca the woman we're supposed to watch over but she's our mate as well," Nicholas whispered, his arms coming up to cradle Rebecca against his chest. Her even breathing told him she was still out cold.

"Maybe our mother knew and that's what she meant by 'you will know her when you join with her'. I had no idea it would feel like that," Darien sighed as he dropped tiredly to the sand next to Nicholas. His gaze moved to Rebecca's face and he reached out to softly stroke her cheek. "Now what do we do?"

"We protect her."

"How? Do you really think she's just going to go with us to England?"

"We're not giving her a choice," Nicholas hissed. "We can't. You know as well as I do Sebastian has intensified his efforts to find her. She's a sitting duck here. We can better protect her at the castle."

"What about her friend?"

Nicholas sighed and ran his fingers through Rebecca's hair, subconsciously holding her closer. He'd almost forgotten about the young woman who'd come with her. If Rebecca disappeared Tonya could be a real problem, bringing attention where they least wanted it.

"I don't know," he whispered. "We'll think of something."

* * * * *

Tonya stared at the ceiling, her gaze still blurred and her breathing ragged from the amazing orgasm she'd just had. And with a stranger to boot. Hell of a fantasy. Her lips spread into a grin.

"I think I'm in love with you," she teased, bringing her hand up to tangle in his short black hair.

His face was buried in her chest and his chuckle shook both of them. "You just think?" he teased back. "I must have been a little off then."

She laughed then slapped at his shoulder. "Someone is going to come out here and see us."

"Let them," he murmured then licked at her breasts, making her shiver in renewed desire.

"Oooh, that feels good," she whispered. His cock began to harden again inside her, warming her flesh. "Insatiable monster," she hissed then laughed when he bit down gently on her nipple. "I can't believe I just did this," she said, more to the ceiling than anyone in particular.

Marcus chuckled and rose up on his palms to smile down at her. His grin deepened the lines around his eyes and she reached up to gently trace one. There was a look of possessiveness in his gaze that startled her and she held her breath, wondering why it thrilled her like it did. Narrowing her eyes, she tried to think of something else. The last thing she needed to do was fall for a man she'd only meant to be a one-night stand and that's all this was.

He'd probably slept with God knows how many women. Why hadn't she thought of that before? My God. They hadn't even used a condom. What had she been thinking? She wasn't like Rebecca. She couldn't just cast a spell and protect herself from pregnancy or anything else for that matter.

His smile faded somewhat as he watched her. "What's wrong?"

"Nothing," she replied quickly. "I was just wondering how old you are."

She wondered at the sudden insecurity that flashed across his gaze. "You wouldn't believe me if I told you."

"Try me," she whispered.

He stared at her for a long moment, gauging her maybe, and she tried to read the emotions shining in his stare. With a devilish grin that made his eyes glow he shook his head. "A man has to have some secrets, sweet."

Tonya snorted. "I always thought it was women that were supposed to be mysterious."

She'd couldn't remember the last time she'd felt so alive, so satisfied, and deep down she hated to let it go. Marcus raised his hand and touched his fingers to her forehead. With a soft smile he slowly dragged his fingers down her face. Her eyes became heavy, tired, and before she realized what had happened she fell fast asleep.

Marcus stared down at the beauty beneath him. Her dark blonde hair and deep green eyes made a heavenly combination and contrasted perfectly with her tan complexion. She was short, maybe about five foot four with curves that made him sweat the second he saw her but there was more to her. She was spunky, fun-loving, sweet.

What he'd felt as they'd joined had been unlike anything he'd felt before. At first it had surprised him that he'd connected so deeply with a mortal. As he was a half-breed vampire he hadn't thought it was possible. Maybe that was something he could thank his mortal white-witch mother for because this was a connection he didn't want to lose.

Sadness filled him as he thought of his mother. He hadn't seen her in over four hundred years. She'd died when he was forty. Two days later his father returned, offering to teach him how to use his vampire powers. His mother had made his father promise to stay away until her death, to give her time at a normal life with her son. Although he hadn't been there physically, he'd supported them financially. A fact he'd found out at his mother's death.

He was an unusual half-breed, something his father loved to point out. He had the immortality and the fangs but lacked the need to feed. Tonight with Tonya had been the first time he'd felt the desire to bite someone, to become a part of them. Although he didn't need blood to survive he could be deadly when provoked and had torn more than one throat of an attacker before getting control of his anger. It was a battle he'd fought hard to win—to keep that devil deeply hidden.

He was also able to tolerate sunlight, which made him what his father's people called a day-walker. It was his mortal blood that allowed the tolerance—the less-than-desirable side of him other vampires either despised or envied.

Something else he'd inherited from his mother had been magical powers. He tended to use magic as opposed to physical strength more often than not, a fact that irritated his father to no end. He didn't like what he became when he unleashed his vampire side.

With a slight smile he reluctantly pulled from Tonya's warm body and adjusted her skirt back over her legs. Tonya didn't yet have the ability to hear his thoughts. He would have to join with her fully—bite her and let her bite him in return—before her mind would meld with his. It was the witch side of him that allowed him to sense her thoughts after sex—it was the witch side that knew she was his life mate.

For a fleeting second he wondered if maybe she had a little witch inside her and just didn't know it. It wasn't unheard of for a natural witch's powers to be suppressed due to lack of training. He also knew from Nicholas and Darien's research on Rebecca that Tonya was an orphan as well.

With a sigh, he wondered how all this with Rebecca would be handled. Tonya could be a problem. Touching his finger to her forehead, he placed memories in her mind of taking a taxi home and climbing into bed. As an afterthought he told her he wanted to see her again. And he did.

Placing a soft kiss on her lips, he blinked and transported her back to her apartment then waited for Nicholas and Darien to emerge from Rebecca's fantasy.

Chapter Four

෨

Rebecca awoke and stretched lazily along the soft sheets beneath her. They felt so good, so much better than what she had at home. Her eyes popped wide open and she stared in confusion at the walls surrounding her. Sitting up, she studied the soft suede wall covering more closely. It looked to be about two shades lighter than the silk comforter covering her chilled and naked body.

A dress lay across the foot of the bed along with underwear and shoes but what held her attention the most were the little windows resembling windows in an airplane. With trembling fingers she threw back the cover and walked the short distance to the window then jumped back with a strangled cry. She was in a plane—a plane in flight to God knew where.

Glancing around for the clothes, she tried to remember what had happened the night before but couldn't. The last thing she remembered was the amazing sex with the identical twins. She stopped short, holding the dress against her chest. Had they kidnapped her? Was that what happened?

Blood pounded through her ears as she quickly threw the dress over her head then slipped on the underwear. Vaguely she realized the flowered material of the underwear matched the dress exactly but she didn't take the time to examine it too closely. The dress didn't require a bra, it had one built in, and she adjusted the underwire before dropping to the bed to slip on the sandals, the whole time keeping her eye on the closed door.

Had they locked it?

Slowly she crept toward it and put her ear to the door. All she could hear was the soft purr of the engines. Licking at her lips, she studied the doorknob, wondering if she should give it a try. If she did get out where would she go? She was flying god knows how many thousands of feet in the air.

"Come out and join us, Rebecca," a deep voice said from the other side of the door and she jumped back, a strangled gasp escaping her parted lips.

The door opened by itself and she stood immobile, staring at the two men from her fantasy. They sat at a table, both dressed in black slacks and black turtlenecks, stretched tight across their wide shoulders.

"We won't bite. At least not hard, anyway," Nicholas said with a devilish grin, sending a wave of heat along her skin. Or at least she thought it was Nicholas. This morning she wasn't exactly sure.

"That's real funny," she snarled, crossing her arms over her chest. "Where are you taking me?"

"Home," the other one said as he stood and strolled toward her. With his hand, he brushed his long black hair over his shoulder. The same hand he'd used to caress her body with such tenderness, such care.

Taking a deep breath, she brushed those memories from her mind. "Somehow I don't think it takes a plane to get me from the club back to my apartment. Where's Tonya?" she demanded.

"She's fine. She's home." The one walking toward her stopped and rested his palm against the wall, his other hand at his hip.

"She'll be looking for me."

"Yes, she will," he said, his lips twitching slightly. "I'm Darien."

"Yes. You told me your names in the club."

She remained rooted to same spot, unsure she wanted to move into the other room with them.

"Come in here and have a seat, Rebecca," Nicholas said and she shook her head.

"I believe I'll remain where I am, Nicholas, thank you."

Darien grinned then glanced at his brother. "She's a stubborn little thing, isn't she?"

"Just like her father."

Her eyes widened and her breath caught in her chest. "You knew my father?"

"Yes," Nicholas said. "Your father and our father were friends."

Her gaze narrowed. "How do I know you're telling the truth?"

"You don't," Darien said, his shoulder lifting in a shrug.

"Exactly," she snapped. "What do you want with me?"

"We promised our father we would protect you," Nicholas offered as he waved his hand toward the couch across from the small table. "Come, Rebecca, please. I'm sure you're hungry. It's way past noon. While you eat we can explain."

Licking her dry lips, she studied Darien and his understanding gaze. Hunger rumbled through her stomach at the mention of food and she grudgingly admitted to herself she could eat. More than twelve hours had passed since the last time she'd eaten and she was starving. "Fine," she snarled, then moved to sit at the couch.

A woman stepped forward quickly, placing a plate of delicate china in her hands laden with fruit, cheese and crackers. On the table next to Rebecca the woman placed a glass of red wine. "How do I know you haven't done anything to it?" she asked, her gaze narrowing on Nicholas.

Nicholas' dark eyes flashed fire then sparkled with amusement. "I could put you to sleep with a wave of my hand, Becca. Why would I need to put anything in your food?"

"It's *Re*becca and what do you mean by put me to sleep with a wave of your hand?"

"We're warlocks, just like you're a witch."

Rebecca choked. Struggling for air, she grabbed her wine and took several sips, finishing off half the glass. Nicholas snapped his fingers and a glass of water appeared in his hand. She stopped breathing, staring at that glass in disbelief.

He leaned forward, taking the wine glass and replacing it with the water. "Drink this. I don't want you drunk because you drank the wine too fast."

Turning the glass in her hand, she glared at it then back at the twins. "How did you do that?"

"That little trick wasn't any different from some of the ones you've done in the past," Darien said as he dropped onto the couch next to her.

"How did you know I was a witch?" she asked, still holding the glass in front of her. "Are we designed to pick each other out of a crowd? Do we have some inner radar that tells us another witch is close by?"

Darien chuckled. "If only it were that simple."

"No, there is no inner radar," Nicholas said, a slight grin tugging at his lips. "How we were able to find you is a little hard explain."

"Try," she said.

"Like we said before, we promised our father we would find and protect you. Our mother cast a spell that would ensure we would know you when we found you. We would know it was you when we…joined with you."

"You're joking, right? What did you have to do? Sleep with every woman you met until you found me?"

Darien snorted then glanced toward the cushions, trying to hide his grin. "No. We saw you at the restaurant. The night you tripped the waiter, making him spill the hot coffee on your date's crotch."

Her face heated as a blush moved over her cheeks.

"Remind me never to make you that angry."

"You saw me do that?" she asked, her voice soft as a whisper, her breath shallow and quick. If they'd seen her, who else had?

"Yes," Nicholas replied. "I was looking at you when you waved your hand. You don't have to do that, by the way."

"I've always done it. I haven't figured out yet how to do it without waving my hand."

"I can teach you," Nicholas said and her heart skipped a beat.

Images of the night before flashed through her mind and her cheeks heated.

"You look a lot like your mother."

Her breath caught and she turned to stare at Darien in surprise. She'd never known her mother. "You knew her too?"

"Yes. We have pictures if you would like to see them, although not on us."

Rebecca shook her head, unsure she should believe any of this. "This is insane. I want to go back home. I have friends, a job…"

"Both have already been taken care of," Nicholas interrupted with a nod.

Her stomach knotted in apprehension. "What do you mean 'taken care of'?" she demanded.

"You sent your job a letter of resignation and you also left a letter for Tonya."

"I did not!" she snapped. "Tonya isn't going to believe that. She knows I would never just leave her a letter." Darien moved closer, putting his hand on her arm but she jerked it away in anger. "Don't touch me!"

"Rebecca," Nicholas chided and she ground her teeth in frustration.

"Don't try to placate me like a damn child," she growled.

"I'm not placating you, damn it!" he yelled, coming to his feet and stretching to his full height, which had to be well over six feet. She swallowed her growing fear and met his glare with one of her own. "We're trying to protect you, Rebecca. From the man who killed your parents. Now that we've joined he'll know you've been found. He won't rest until you're dead. Just like your parents."

Nicholas watched the color drain from her face and regret slammed through him. He shouldn't have yelled at her like that. He should have been more patient. Darien shot him a glare from his seat next to her and Nicholas sighed, wishing he'd been instructed on how to handle this part. With his father dead, he and his brother were on their own.

"I'm sorry, Rebecca," he said quietly and her eyes narrowed in anger. Good. He would much rather see her angry than scared.

"What do you mean he won't rest until I'm dead like my parents? Why did he kill my parents?"

"Your father held a seat on the Witches council. One of the most powerful ones. He found out something about Sebastian—he's the man who killed your parents—but we're not sure what that was. Your father was killed before he could tell anyone."

"What does that have to do with me? Why am I in danger?"

"You've inherited your father's seat and Sebastian wants it. In order to get it he has to provide proof of your death."

"I see," she murmured, then shuddered. "This is…"

"Is what, baby?" Nicholas asked and her startled gaze met his. Had he just called her baby?

"If I hadn't spent the last ten years trying to control my own powers I would have said the two of you were insane."

Nicholas and Darien both laughed.

"This isn't funny," she snapped. "You kidnapped me. Why didn't you just explain it?"

"We didn't have time, Rebecca," Darien replied. "We have no idea where Sebastian is. He could have gotten to you before we had a chance to explain. We had to move fast."

Rebecca finally placed the glass of water on the table beside her, her brow drawn in a thoughtful expression. "Tonya will be beside herself. She'll know I didn't leave that letter." She looked at Nicholas and the sadness he saw darkening her eyes made his gut clench. "I can't just leave her hanging. And what if Sebastian thinks to use her to get to me?"

"He shouldn't even know about Tonya," Nicholas said.

"Why wouldn't he? According to you, once the three of us join, he'll know. Who's to say he won't find out about me and about my friends?" She raised her hand, slapping them down on her thighs. "And why in God's name would someone cast such a spell? You have to have sex with me to know it's me?"

"It wasn't just about...identifying you," Darien said with a slight grimace. "You are to be our wife."

She raised an eyebrow and glared at them skeptically. "Your wife?"

"Yes," Darien said, his lips lifting in a sideways grin of apology. "Warlocks and witches know their mates when they have sex with them. Apparently our mother knew you would be our life mate and that's why she said we would know you when we joined with you."

"We have a ring if you would like it," Darien offered and she stared at him in shock.

"What I would like," she snapped, "is for the two of you to come back to reality. Your wife? Okay. I may believe the warlock story but your *wife*?"

"Why is that so hard to fathom?" Nicholas asked in exasperation. He would never understand women. "This is how it's always done within our kind. Warlock to witch. It's what keeps us pure."

She snorted. "Pure? And what if you fall in love with a mortal?"

"There have been a few," Darien relented. "But not many. Is becoming our wife so distasteful? Did we not go well together?"

An adorable pink blush moved over her cheeks. "That's not the point. I might be okay with the whole protection thing. But I refuse to marry you."

Nicholas started to say something but Darien held up his hand, stopping him. "We will agree to that for now. But at least give us the opportunity to change your mind."

"You want the opportunity to court me?" she asked

Darien shrugged and Nicholas almost laughed out loud at her shocked expression. She was so damn adorable. "No," Nicholas replied, his grin widening. "We just want you to keep an open mind."

She snorted, crossing her arms over her chest.

"Think about it. If the sex was that good, imagine what day-to-day life would be like."

"Let's see," she murmured. "Going from uncontrollable lust to wanting to strangle you? Yeah, I can see how that would make for a heck of a day-to-day life." She rolled her eyes. "I want to contact Tonya. That's the only way you'll get my cooperation."

"You're not exactly in a position to be making demands, Becca," Darien replied, his lips forming a lopsided grin.

"Wanna bet?" she snarled and raised her hands to snap her fingers. Nicholas reached out and grasped her hands within his, making her eyes narrow dangerously.

"Don't be foolish, Rebecca. You're not strong enough to transport yourself that far," Nicholas hissed.

Rebecca watched him, studied him as though trying to read his mind. *You know I'm right,* he whispered into her mind and her eyes widened in fear.

"You can speak to me in my mind?" she whispered.

"Yes and you will be able to speak to us that way, as well, once you fully accept your fate. Now promise to behave and we'll see that you get to speak to Tonya. Deal?"

"You said I was too far away to transport myself. Where are you taking me?"

"England," Darien replied and her face went ashen.

* * * * *

Tonya stood outside the door to the club and banged her knuckles loudly against the wood. There was no way Rebecca would leave and not explain it in person. Sunshine beat down on her bare shoulders, warming her as the morning moved into afternoon. She'd slept for over ten hours, awakening to find Rebecca's note that she'd left with the men in her fantasy. Something was wrong. She knew it deep in her gut.

Her patience wore thin and her shoes tapped out an angry rhythm against the sidewalk. After seconds of waiting for a response she rapped her knuckles against the door again, this time a little louder.

The door opened and she stared angrily at the woman who greeted her. "Where's Marcus?" Tonya demanded.

"He's..." the woman began until a tall form moved to stand behind her.

Marcus.

Tonya's heart began to beat fast in her chest as she stared at the gorgeous man who'd given her the best sex of her life just hours before. "Where is she?" Tonya demanded, trying to keep her mind on the task at hand.

"Who?" he asked innocently, nodding to the confused woman who'd first answered the door. She walked away, leaving her with an amused Marcus.

"Don't act all innocent with me, damn it. I'm talking about Rebecca. The woman I came in here with yesterday."

"Oh yes. Rebecca. I have no idea." He shrugged and Tonya mentally stomped down the urge to smack him.

Tonya put her hands on her hips and glared up at him. "You had to have seen them leave. Or were you having sex with someone else?"

He smiled slightly, his eyes sparkling with merriment. "Jealous?"

"Oh for the love of," she sighed, rolling her eyes. "As if. You were a fantasy fuck, hotshot, get over it."

"Oh I think I was more than just a fantasy fuck, don't you?" With a sexy as hell grin he leaned against the doorjamb and crossed his arms over his very wide chest.

She waved the note she held in her hand. "I'm here to find out about my friend, not argue with you over what type of sex it was. Now…are you going to help me or am I going to go to the police?"

"She's an adult, Tonya. Can't she leave if she so chooses?"

"Of course she can. That's not the point. The point is how she did it. She would never have just left me a note. Nor would she have left without her stuff. She didn't take anything."

Marcus sighed then glanced toward the sky, his eyes squinting at the bright sunlight. "I'm sure you'll hear from her soon."

"I give up," she sighed with a wave of her hand. "Fine."

She turned to head back down the sidewalk and hail a cab to take her to the police department. Marcus jumped from the doorway and moved much faster than any man should be able to. Before she got two steps away he stood in front of her, blocking her path. Her stomach flipped in surprise as she stared up at his height in anger.

"What are you doing?" she snapped.

"Come inside and I'll make a few phone calls," he replied. "I'm sure there's no need to get the police involved. Besides, I doubt they would listen to you anyway."

Her gaze narrowed. "So you know who took her?"

"I'm not saying that but I'm sure I can find out."

Tonya pursed her lips, hoping she wasn't about to make a huge mistake. But something deep inside made her think she could trust him—made her think she could believe what he said. Taking a deep breath, she nodded in agreement.

"Fine," she said, waving her hand toward the massive double doors of the club. "Lead the way."

Marcus' lips twitched slightly in amusement but she didn't miss the hint of worry in his gaze and it increased her trepidation as she followed him inside the darkened interior. He made his way to the back of the room and through another set of double doors that lead to the back offices, Tonya close on his heels.

Without warning he turned to face her, making her screech to a halt. "Stay here," he ordered and her mouth dropped open in surprise.

"I don't think so."

"Stay here or no deal," he demanded, then turned to step into an office.

The door didn't shut all the way and she leaned closer so she could see through the crack. He made his way to the desk then stood studying the phone for countless seconds. What was he doing? Pretending to make a phone call? After a deep sigh he picked up the receiver but instead of dialing the number he waved his hand across the keypad.

Tonya's eyes narrowed in anger but she remained outside the door, listening.

* * * * *

Nicholas' cell phone beeped, making Rebecca jump. She stared at the device speculatively as he lifted it from his belt holder. "That thing works on the plane?" she asked, staring at him skeptically. "I thought once you're above so many thousand feet they don't work."

"Magic," Nicholas mouthed and almost laughed at her expression of disbelief. Flipping the phone open, he spoke into the mouthpiece. "Marcus. What is it?"

"It's Tonya. She's going to be a problem. Hell, not going to be. *Is* a problem."

"What happened?" Nicholas asked as he stood and walked into the bedroom for privacy.

"She's here at the club, demanding answers. She thinks I know who took Rebecca and insists she'll go to the police if she doesn't get what she wants."

"Oh boy," Nicholas sighed, then glanced back at Rebecca, who watched him with suspicion. "Well, take care of it."

"How?" Marcus demanded.

"You like her. Bring her to the castle."

"You can't be serious."

"It will solve two problems. Yours and the one I'm having with Rebecca."

"Son of a bitch," Marcus sighed. "Fine. I'll take care of her."

* * * * *

Marcus hung up the phone and glanced up in surprise to see Tonya standing in the doorway, her eyes wide as saucers. Anger surged through him—anger at himself. He should have heard her, seen her, something. For a brief second he wondered if maybe he'd wanted her to hear.

His body tensed as her fear wrapped around his heart. She was going to run, he could see it in her thoughts.

"Tonya," he cautioned, then cursed when she spun around, taking off at a run down the hallway and toward the front part of the club.

He sprinted after her, using his enhanced speed to catch her quickly and wrap his arms around her waist, trapping her against him. She struggled, kicking her legs and swinging her arms wildly.

"Let me go, you damn son of a bitch," she squealed.

"No," he snapped. "You wanted to see Rebecca and you're going to."

"What?" she gasped. "Where is she? What have you done to her?"

"I haven't done anything to her, Tonya, I promise," he spoke softly in her ear, trying to calm her down. "Listen to me."

"Why should I?" she murmured, her voice shaking slightly.

He could feel her fear, her anger, and it cut like a knife in his chest. She was his one—his mate—and he hated that their relationship would start out like this.

"Because you know you can trust me. Deep down you *know* it."

She stopped struggling, her harsh breathing the only sound in the quiet room. He loosened his hold slightly, allowing her to turn in his embrace. Her eyes were wide, fear and uncertainty clouding their depths, her cheeks flushed with anger. Her uncertainty filled him, made him want to protect her, make her see that he would never hurt her.

He brushed his thumb across her forehead then set his fingers over her eyes, sliding them down her face slowly. Her eyes began to droop as her body went limp in his arms, falling asleep just as he wanted her to.

"You know you can trust me," he whispered.

Chapter Five

Rebecca sat on the edge of Tonya's bed, waiting for her to open her eyes. She still hadn't come to even though it had been over an hour since she and Marcus had arrived. The castle sat nestled among the trees with a beautiful lake behind it. Although they were technically in England, Nicholas informed her they were in a protected dimension. One they hoped would keep her secure from Sebastian until they could find out where he was and what his next move might be.

Marcus had come by twice to check on Tonya. She'd been told all about Marcus before he arrived—about who and what he was. She'd always thought vampires were a fairy tale born from someone's dark imagination. In the few short hours she'd been here she'd learned of other fairy tales that weren't just tales.

The obvious concern in Marcus' gaze as he watched Tonya melted Rebecca's heart toward the half-breed vampire. The fact that he had feelings for her friend was apparent but how did Tonya feel? Seeing she was still asleep, Marcus left the room, leaving her alone with her friend.

Tonya stirred, a soft whimper escaping her lips. Rebecca placed her hand on her shoulder, shaking her gently. "Tonya," she whispered and her friend sat upright instantly, her gaze flicking around the room in fear.

"What happened?" she gasped then her eyes landed on Rebecca. "Oh my god, are you okay? Where are we?"

"One question at a time," Rebecca said with a laugh. "As to what happened, Marcus put you in a trance but you were out for quite a while, much longer than he expected, and I'm afraid he's terribly worried."

"Marcus can go to hell," Tonya snapped. "He put me in a trance? The last thing I remember is him touching my-my face," she added with a whisper. "Is that how he did it? Dragging his fingers down my face?"

Rebecca shrugged. "I don't know."

"Where are we?"

"Well, we're sort of in England."

"How can you be 'sort of' in England?" Tonya asked with a frown. "And what do they want with you? With us?"

"It's hard to explain but it's me they wanted. They only took you because you threatened to go to the police." Tonya opened her mouth to speak but Rebecca held up her hand. "I'm fine, I promise. They haven't harmed me and I don't believe they will."

"But why did they take you?"

"It has to do with my parents," Rebecca whispered and handed her the photos the twins had given her earlier.

Darien had been right. She did look like her mother but she had a little of her father in her too. Tonya studied the pictures then looked at Rebecca with confusion. "I still don't understand."

"Neither do I, at least not completely. Apparently a man by the name of Sebastian killed my parents in order to gain control of my father's seat on the Witches council—"

Tonya coughed then held up her hand. "I'm sorry. Witches council?"

"I know. It sounds like something off of Bewitched but I believe them. They're warlocks, Tonya. Much more powerful than me. They claim they were sent to find and protect me from Sebastian. According to them I have inherited my father's seat and their father hid me. Sebastian can't get that seat until he produces proof of my death."

"Oh my god," Tonya gasped then rubbed at her forehead with a frown. "This is nuts."

"Headache?"

"Yeah."

"Marcus said you might. He told me if you did to let him know and he'd take care of it."

Tonya shook her head. "No. I-I'm not ready to see him just yet. He unsettles me."

Glancing at her friend, Tonya tried to read her eyes—tried to see if Rebecca were really okay with all this. Tonya wasn't. At least not yet. How had Marcus gotten her here so quickly? And what did Tonya do about how she felt whenever Marcus was near?

"So back to this 'sort of' thing," Tonya said, trying to change the subject from Marcus.

"We're in what's called a protected dimension."

"A what?" Tonya asked, raising an eyebrow in disbelief.

"Remember the Harry Potter movies? Well it's like that in a way. It's England but not really England. You have to go to England to get here but—"

Tonya held up a hand, stopping her. "Can you tell you're somewhere else? Just by looking around?"

Rebecca nodded then stood. Tonya watched her, nervousness pulling her stomach into knots as her friend walked over to the maroon velvet curtains and pulled them apart. Sunlight streamed through the French doors, warming the hardwood floor and illuminating the previously darkened room.

Rebecca motioned her over to the window. "Perhaps you should see for yourself."

With a deep breath, Tonya climbed from the bed and placed her bare feet against the cool floor. She still wore her jeans and blue tank tank from when she'd confronted Marcus and the cool air of the room sent goose bumps along her bare arms.

Standing, she slowly made her way to the doors as Rebecca opened them. "This is the second floor balcony. It spans the entire length of the back of the castle and overlooks the gardens below. I think you'll find what's in the gardens rather interesting."

Scowling at her friend, Tonya stepped through and forward to the iron railing. The weather was warm, almost springlike. The gardens were full of flowering shrubs and flowers the likes of which she'd never seen, colors so bright and full they looked as though they'd been painted by the strokes of an artist's brush.

Her intrigued gaze wandered along the garden paths to a clearing close to a lake. Her breath caught in her throat as she stared at what she had initially thought to be horses. But they weren't horses.

She raised her hand to point. "Are those?"

"Unicorns?" Rebecca asked, a grin tugging at her lips. "Yes. There's also a pegasus." With a nod, she pointed out the horse flying across the horizon, his wings spread wide, his legs curled beneath him.

"This can't be real. These things are from Greek mythology. What the hell are they doing here?"

"They're here for protection. Have been for thousands of years. I haven't seen them but there are also a couple of dragons and a few other things I hadn't ever heard of before. I should probably warn you about Vincent as well."

"Who's Vincent?" Tonya asked with trepidation, unsure she even wanted to know. This whole trip had turned into a bad version of Fantasy Island.

"Vincent is—"

"Me," a deep voice rumbled from behind her.

"You could have at least given me a moment to prepare her, Vincent," Rebecca chided.

Tonya slowly turned her head, almost afraid to look. At first she didn't see anything and frowned toward the empty room. With a shrug, she glanced back to Rebecca.

"Down here, my dear," the deep voice said, a soft English accent punctuating his words.

Her gaze dropped to the floor and she stared in shock at a cat. His tail swishing gently, his fur a rich deep black, his eyes so blue they rivaled the sky outside. A diamond-studded collar decorated his neck and sparkled as he tilted his head slightly to study her. Tonya's heart skipped a beat. She would swear he smiled at her.

"What's wrong, dear? Cat got your tongue?" Vincent asked in amusement.

Tonya opened her lips to speak but nothing came out. The room began to rock precariously and she grabbed the railing to keep from falling but it was no use. Darkness closed in around her and she fell straight into Rebecca's arms.

"That went well," Vincent drawled and Rebecca shot him a glare.

"You did that on purpose, you mean old cat," she snapped.

"Now why would I have done that?" he purred.

"According to Nicholas, because you enjoy it." Rebecca huffed softly as she positioned Tonya's limp body onto one of the wicker lounge chairs along the balcony.

"You shouldn't believe everything he tells you, Rebecca. Nicholas tends to exaggerate things, especially when they pertain to me."

Rebecca rolled her eyes. She'd already had to come between Nicholas and the cat once today. She wasn't sure who enjoyed antagonizing the other more, Nicholas or Vincent. "Go get Marcus, Vincent. Please."

Vincent meowed then took off. Rebecca sighed, wondering if maybe she should have handled the explanations better. She still hadn't wrapped her mind around everything yet herself. She still felt as though she was trapped in some sort of dream. The twins were another problem.

Her attraction to them plagued her. More than once since they'd arrived she'd found herself replaying that night at the club. She couldn't stop thinking about it, about how what Nicholas and Darien felt had slammed into her, mixing with her own sensations. It had been intense and overwhelming.

She'd wanted to ask if it would always be like that but had been too embarrassed. Just thinking about having sex with them again kept her awake, made her pussy ache with the need to feel them again. It was like a drug addiction—strong and undeniable. But it wasn't just the sex she was addicted to. It was the twins. Just spending time with them made her feel happy—happier then she'd felt in a long time.

Tonya stirred and Rebecca placed a hand on her arm. "You okay?" she asked.

Her friend cracked open one eye. "Is it gone?"

"Yes," Rebecca said with a nod, her lips twitching slightly at Tonya's obvious trepidation.

"What was that?"

"That was Vincent. He's Nicholas and Darien's great, great uncle. Serving out a few decades as a cat is the punishment inflicted on him by the council. Apparently he was a roguish warlock. He seduced someone he wasn't supposed to." Tonya snorted then covered her mouth with her hand to stifle a giggle. "I know. This whole thing is outlandish, isn't it?"

Tonya nodded, laughter now rumbling through her chest. "Who are Nicholas and Darien? Aren't they the men from the club?" she asked once she'd settled down.

"Yes."

Tonya's eyes narrowed. "They had that dog take your keys on purpose didn't they?"

"Actually." Rebecca looked down at her nails. "Nicholas *was* the dog."

"*What?*"

"Feeling better?" Marcus asked from the open doorway.

Rebecca didn't miss the heat flaring in Tonya's eyes before she tamped it down, anger taking its place as she glared at Marcus. "Go easy on him," Rebecca whispered. "He's been beside himself, worried about you."

Tonya snorted, unsure she believed that load of crap.

"I'll leave the two of you alone," Rebecca murmured and Tonya reached out to grasp her hand. She didn't want to be alone with him. She knew what would happen if she were.

"You'll be fine," Rebecca whispered then pulled her hand free. "I'll check on you later."

With that her friend left the room, leaving her alone with a man she both lusted after and hated. Crossing her arms over her chest, Tonya glared at Marcus in silence.

"You must be feeling better. You're shooting daggers at me."

His lips spread into an adorable smile, lighting up his deep blue eyes and making them sparkle. Tingles ran down her spine but she brushed them aside, ignoring the affect his nearness had on her senses.

"I should be shooting bullets," she snarled.

"You wanted to see Rebecca," he reasoned.

"You kidnapped me."

He waved his hand, dismissing it and shooting her the most sensual smile she'd ever seen. Her flesh heated from the inside out.

"Details," he purred.

"That's a big detail, Marcus. You scared me. I thought you were going to go all mob on me and dump my ass in the river."

Marcus shook his head with an amused frown. "No, sweet. I don't dump people in the river anymore. They have a tendency of floating back up. Now I just cut them up into little pieces and feed them to the dragons."

Tonya narrowed her gaze. "You're such an ass."

Laughter rumbled through his chest as he came further out onto the balcony. He wore all black again but it looked good on him. The black slacks accentuated his trim waist, the black t-shirt hugged his muscular chest. Flashes of that afternoon at the club went through her mind and without thinking her gaze dropped to his cock, which she could see outlined behind the zipper of his pants.

As though reading her mind he asked softly, "Are you sure you're up for that?"

Her gaze shot back to his and the heat of a blush moved over her neck. "Excuse me?"

"You were staring at my crotch as though you were starving."

"Don't be ridiculous."

He smiled and her stomach flipped. Juices poured from her pussy as she imagined the two of them in that huge bed just a few feet away. What was wrong with her? Why couldn't she stop thinking about it—wanting it?

"I'm sorry I frightened you."

He said it with such sincerity her gut clenched and she became even angrier with herself, which came out toward him.

"You should be!" she snapped and jumped up from the lounge chair. With hands on her hips, she glared at him. "You can't just put women in a trance and take them wherever the hell you want. You know you can go to jail for this, right? You know what you did is illegal?"

"You know you're cute when you're pissed," he teased.

"Screw you," she snapped and he raised an eyebrow as though she'd just challenged him.

Marcus slowly stalked toward her, backing her toward the room as he advanced. Her heart raced at the animal lust shining in his gaze—the way his muscles rippled beneath his shirt as he moved ever closer. His masculine scent mingled with the sweet smell of the flowers below, heating her skin and mentally drawing her to him like a moth to a burning flame.

"How do you ever expect me to—"

Marcus' mouth covered hers so fast she didn't have time to prepare—to stop him. But the second his scent invaded her nostrils and wrapped around her she found she didn't want to stop him. His lips were firm and hard at first then softened to glide enticingly across hers. Her mouth parted, allowing him access to deepen the kiss and invade her with his wicked tongue. He tasted so good—like coffee mixed with caramel— and she sucked at his tongue to get every last flavor.

He moaned into her kiss, his arms encircling her waist to pull her close. Her breasts pressed against his chest, his palms splayed against the small of her back, sending shocks of electricity through her limbs. With a desperate moan her fingers clenched and unclenched within the fabric of his shirt, her nails scraping his chest through the material.

She felt possessed. Every part of her screamed to take him—to let him take her. She needed him as much as she needed water to drink and the realization sent shock waves through her body.

Warm fingers moved beneath the fabric of her shirt, connecting with her flesh to scorch her very soul. His touch set her on fire, made her crazy with lust. One hand moved around to cup her breasts and she cried out, the sound swallowed by his kiss—a never-ending kiss that consumed her. If she didn't get his flesh against hers, didn't get his cock buried inside her soon, she'd combust—fall to the floor in a pile of ash.

Marcus tugged at her top, breaking the kiss just long enough for him to remove it, letting the fabric fall to the floor forgotten. Cool air brushed across her nipples only to be replaced by the warmth of his lips as he teased her sensitive nubs. Her fingers buried in his hair, tugging him closer, begging for more of his delicious torture.

"Marcus," she sighed. "What are you doing to me?"

"Whatever you want me to do, sweet," he purred then tugged at the buttons of her jeans, ripping the material.

She gasped, her pussy spasming and leaking cream. She wanted him so bad it defied understanding. Only a moment ago she'd hated him. Now she couldn't seem to get enough of him—couldn't seem to get him close enough.

With an animalistic growl that sent her heart into palpitations, he lifted her onto the dresser and tugged her jeans off, throwing them across the room. Next went his shirt and her hands immediately moved to skim across his hard flesh. His lips covered hers as he pulled her hips close, his hard cock grinding against her hungry mound through the material of his pants.

It wasn't enough and she groaned in frustration, desperate to feel his thick cock filling her. Her hands moved to his fly, tugging it apart with the same hungry desperation he'd used on hers. They both worked to shove his pants to the floor, where he hurriedly kicked them aside.

With his hands gripping her ass, he lifted her so her legs could encircle his waist as he walked back into the bedroom. She ground her pussy then held on tight to his shoulders to lift herself slightly. With a long, low growl she sank her pussy down onto his pulsing shaft, taking him clear to her womb.

They didn't make it to the bed. Instead he shoved her against the wall, pushing his cock even deeper. His mouth covered hers, swallowing her cries of delight as he pounded into her, sending her senses reeling out of control. Pinned to the wall as she was she couldn't move with him but had to take what he gave her. And what he gave her was heaven. She could feel every delectable inch of his shaft as he moved in and out, his cock stretching her with every pounding thrust into her pussy.

His grunts mingled with her cries as his thrusts became even more powerful, demanding even more from her. He bit at the sensitive flesh below her ear, his teeth gently scraping across her skin. Something pricked her then a trickle of warm fluid slid down her neck.

The slight bite of pain only intensified her pleasure and her orgasm slammed through her instantly. She screamed, holding tight to Marcus as he pressed deep, grinding his pelvis against her clit, intensifying her pleasure until he too stiffened. Pulling away from her neck, he reared his head back and growled, shoving himself into her hard, spilling his warm seed into her pulsing channel.

"You're mine, Tonya," he growled and she opened her eyes to stare at him in dazed wonderment. "Only mine."

Blood coated his lips and she rubbed her finger across it in confusion. Lifting her hand, she touched the side of her neck and winced at the sharp bite of pain. His eyes widened slightly then filled with concern. Pulling her hand away from her neck, she stared in shock at the blood on her fingers.

Their gazes met and locked as realization dawned for Tonya. "What did you do?" she whispered.

Keeping her pinned to the wall with his hips, he lifted his hands to cup her face. "I'm sorry, sweet. You weren't ready for this."

"For what?" she croaked.

Fear raced through her veins and she would have run if given the chance. Now that her vision had cleared somewhat she could see his fangs. *Fangs? What the hell?* Reaching out, she touched one, feeling the sharp tip. She pulled her hand away as though burned. As she watched they slowly receded but the magnitude of what had just happened still hung between them.

"You've become a part of me," he whispered.

Her heart stopped then sped out of control. What did he mean a part of him? Was he a vampire? Was that even possible? "Let me down."

"No." He put his palms against the wall, holding her in place. "Not until we talk."

She gritted her teeth, shooting daggers at him as he stared down at her. "Then talk. What are you?"

"I'm half vampire, half warlock. I'm what they call a day walker."

"What about feeding? Aren't vampires supposed to feed on the blood of others? Is that what you just did to me?"

"I don't need to feed, not like a normal vampire. But the urge to bite intensifies when I'm with my true mate."

Her eyes widened. "Your what?"

"My mate. You, Tonya."

Removing one hand from the wall, he held a warm washcloth before her face, his eyebrow raised in question. She nodded slightly, her body tense. She held herself as stiff as possible as he gently placed it against the side of her neck.

"Where did you get that?" she whispered.

"Half witch, remember?" he replied, an apologetic smile tugging at his lips. "You shouldn't fear me, sweet. I would never hurt you."

She snorted but kept her gaze glued to his. She felt awkward, his cock still buried inside her, her breasts still pressed against his chest. Awkward didn't even begin to cover it. She'd just had sex with a vampire. What was she saying? There was no such thing!

She shifted slightly, forcing his cock deeper, and closed her eyes in a mixture of aggravation and desire.

"Keep doing that and you'll get a repeat performance."

"The hell I will," she snarled. "You're supposed to be talking, remember? Did you make me into you?"

He shook his head. "No. At least not yet. That's your decision to make."

"If I said yes. Then what?"

"You would feed from me and become what I am. A half-breed. Half human, half vampire. We would lack the need to feed but still have the capacity. I have been known to bite or draw blood when defending myself but have never done it for a need of food. I can eat normal meals, just like you. I can walk around during the day but I am immortal. I also have the ability to read your mind due to my warlock side. If we were to join completely you would be what I am."

"This is nuts."

"No, sweet. It's real. I felt the desire to bite you the other night at the club but I suppressed it. I guess today just got a little out of hand."

Staring into his beautiful eyes, she swallowed. She believed him. Everything he told her. How had her life changed so quickly? One minute she was a normal person with a normal job then suddenly she was in a castle somewhere in "sort of" England with a talking cat and a half-breed vampire. *Oh my God. I've lost my damn mind.*

Chapter Six

80

Rebecca strolled through the library, her fingers running delicately along the spines of novels that had to be hundreds of years old. One several shelves up, its leather bindings soft with age, caught her interest and she reached up mentally, tugging the book from its resting spot. It floated slowly toward her hand until she was able to reach out and grab it

"Very good, Becca."

She lifted her gaze to stare at the man who'd spoken. One of the twins stood in the doorway, his arms crossed over his chest, his hip leaning against the door frame. He looked quite dashing and way too sexy for his own good. Unfortunately she didn't know which one he was.

"Darien," he said with a grin.

"The two of you are identical. It's very hard to tell you apart."

Raising his hand, he slid two fingers down his hair on one side, a white stripe appearing in their wake. She frowned then laughed at his attempt to appear different.

"Better?" he asked.

"Much, thank you," she said with a grin. "I think I like it, actually. It gives you a dangerous look for some reason."

"Maybe I'll keep it then." He shrugged. "At least this way you can tell us apart."

She chuckled and moved to sit on the large red sofa facing the massive stone fireplace. "That would certainly be helpful."

Keeping her eyes downcast, she tried to not think about how incredibly sexy he looked in his jeans, a white t-shirt stretched tight across his chest. The blue suede shirt he wore over it accentuated his eyes and made him appear more like a casual rancher than the lord of a mystical castle.

Shouldn't she be getting to know them before jumping their bones every time they looked at her?

"Are you beginning to feel a little more comfortable around me and Nicholas?"

She almost jumped at how close he sounded and stiffened when he sat down on the couch beside her. He had been so quiet she hadn't even heard him approach. With a shrug, she kept her gaze on the book in her hand. Opening the worn, tattered pages, she studied the writing, which had faded with age.

"I suppose. Why do you ask?"

"Because I'm dying to lay you across this couch and screw the hell out of you."

Her head came up with a jerk and tingles of desire skimmed along her flesh. She stared at him with a mixture of shock and anger—anger with herself for immediately coming to a state of burning need with his brash words. Heat flared in his eyes as he met her gaze and she swallowed, trying hard to think of a biting retort, but not a damn thing would come to mind. She was utterly speechless.

"You're nothing if not blunt," she snapped, making him grin.

He gently brushed the hair from her eyes, making her skin tingle. "I don't see any sense in mincing words, not when I can sense your needs as clear as I can sense my own."

"Where's Nicholas?" she asked, trying to change the subject from the dangerous path it headed down.

Her whole body tingled with lust. Even her nipples were not immune as the material of her bra brushed against them, making them harden and ache for his touch. She did want him. More than anything right now she wanted him to do exactly as he'd said and it scared her to death. She'd never felt this kind of attraction and wondered just how real it was. Was it a spell? And if so, did she want a relationship based on that?

"He's in the lab with Vincent. They're trying to formulate a spell that will draw out Sebastian as well as a protection spell for you. Prefer the two of us as opposed to just one?" he purred, reaching out to tug at one of the curls dangling around her earlobe.

"Stop it," she whispered.

He only grinned, which fueled her aggravation even more. She needed some breathing room to better understand her jumbled emotions. Darien, in a word, was irresistible. Full, soft lips that could melt any arguments she might have, sultry eyes that could send her into a full state of lust with just a look and of course that amazing body and the confident way he carried it. Even just leaning against the wall he was delectable.

"I need some answers, Darien, not teasing," she pleaded, trying her best to keep her wits about her.

"All right," he conceded with a nod, moving his hand away from her and giving her a much needed reprieve from his overbearing sexuality. "What do you want to know?"

"You've told me so much about my parents, I'm still trying to process everything. My father was very powerful, apparently so was my mother. I'm not by any stretch of the imagination as powerful. How can I fight Sebastian?"

"You won't have to fight him alone. Nicholas and I will be with you. If the three of us combine our powers we'll be able to defeat him."

"Why doesn't someone just kill him?" she asked in exasperation.

"It's not that simple. He's woven several protection spells around himself. Killing him will be a challenge."

Rebecca sighed and closed the book with a loud clap. Insecurities washed through her. Fear gripped her chest. She had trouble doing simple things. How the hell was she

71

supposed to be the woman to save the council from an evil warlock?

"I'm not ready for this," she sighed. "I'm not."

"Hey," Darien murmured as he gripped her chin and turned her to face him. "You won't be alone. I promise." Leaning forward, he placed a soft kiss on her cheek, making her stomach flip. His lips were warm and as he pulled away she caught the scents of mint and tea. "How about we go outside and practice a little? Get those powers of yours warmed up a bit?"

Rebecca smiled slightly as she tried to recapture some of her composure. Just that one simple little kiss had sent her senses into a tailspin. For a fleeting second she could have sworn she felt his need for her, his desire to feel her beneath him, his tension-filled body coiled like a spring. Maybe magic practice was what they both needed to cool off.

With a nod, she relented. "Sounds like a good idea."

* * * * *

Nicholas stood back and watched Rebecca try to manipulate a boulder with magic. Twice she growled in frustration when the rock turned into something other than what she wanted it to. With a chuckle, he leaned against the tree, watching the sunlight play across her face. The pink sundress accentuated her trim waist and firm breasts. The color even brought out her tan and highlighted the blonde in her hair.

Her beauty sometimes left him breathless, incapable of coherent speech. He'd expected the physical bond to be strong but not the emotional one. He never expected he might actually be able to fall in love with his chosen wife but damned if he wasn't halfway there. He loved her spunk. It was no doubt she was a handful.

"Try it this way," Darien explained and for the first time Nicholas noticed the white streak down the side of his hair and smiled slightly.

For Rebecca, he imagined, so she could tell them apart. Not a bad idea really, just unusual for Darien. Normally Darien couldn't care less if people were able to tell them apart. Their family and closest friends could and those were all that mattered.

Rebecca tried again, this time turning the rock into a turtle. "Oh for the love of god," she grumbled, making Nicholas chuckle.

"Poor thing," Vincent purred from his spot on the tree branch several feet off the ground. "I haven't seen magic that bad since... Well I can't remember *ever* seeing magic that bad."

"Give her time. Remember, she hasn't had any formal training. She'll get the hang of it."

"Mmmm," Vincent murmured then flicked his tail. "Let's just hope it's before the Dominion Ball. Are you sure presenting her there is a good idea, Nicholas?"

"Sebastian will be there."

"I'm sure he's already aware of her existence and the fact that you've joined with her."

"I am too but he can't get to her here, it's protected. We also can't keep her here forever. The ball is the best place to bring her out and challenge Sebastian."

Vincent jumped from his perch to the branch closest to Nicholas' shoulder. "Make sure you know what you're doing, Nicholas. Watch your back and keep your eyes open. Something isn't right with Sebastian. It goes beyond evil. There's something we're not aware of. I can feel it in every bone of my body."

* * * * *

Sebastian paced the cold stones of Jullian's castle in Romania, careful to keep his feet in the shadows and not let them hit the part of the floor bathed in the last remains of the evening sunset. He'd kept his vampire transformation hidden for over three hundred years, blaming black magic for his immortality. It wasn't unusual for warlocks to use such spells. Even those pain-in-the-ass twins Nicholas and Darien had dabbled in the black arts — all in the effort to hide Rebecca.

But he had his own methods and sooner or later he'd find her. He needed her family's seat. Once that last seat was filled by Vlad, vampires would once again control the council and in turn everything else, including the mortal world.

"What's got you in such a snit? You're pacing a worn spot in my floor."

Sebastian turned to stare at his friend Jullian as he entered the room. Jullian's long black hair draped around his shoulders, his blue eyes intelligent and dark. Jullian was a strong asset. Despite the fact he kept out of council business he still held a huge amount of influence, if for no other reason than most of the council feared him.

So did he at times.

"Just anxious to get started. I'm hungry."

Jullian nodded and handed him a glass of warm blood. "This will tide you over."

Lifting the glass, Sebastian inhaled the spicy scent of warm blood. He hissed, for a moment allowing the hunger to flow through him. His fangs formed and he curled his lip, running his tongue over the sharp edges of his vampire teeth. Lifting the glass he drank the blood, letting its warmth sooth his lust, calm his hunger. Later tonight he and Jullian would feed, calming his blood lust for a few weeks until it would rise again.

He needed to find Rebecca soon. Make her death look like an accident, or better yet a suicide, then claim her family's seat by right of lineage. He was the closest relative to her father's line. Since Rebecca was the last of the age-old family the line would die with her.

Sebastian smiled as he thought about how close he was to his long-awaited plan coming together. Letting Jullian turn him all those years ago had been a brilliant idea. Of course the fact that they'd been lovers hadn't hurt matters. He and Jullian both enjoyed women, most of the time together—giving them a night of unsurpassed pleasure before feeding from them, quieting their hunger with their blood.

Jullian insisted they not take all of their victims' blood. They had to leave enough for them to survive. The women remembered little beyond the sex and it kept the villages from being too suspicious. His friend was cautious with the women, keeping himself detached, cold.

In all the years he'd known Jullian only one woman had penetrated that cold stone he called a heart. But in the end she'd chosen to remain human, been unwilling to cross over, leaving Jullian broken and angry.

Sebastian turned back to him. His gaze wandered aimlessly over a strong back and firm ass. His cock hardened as he imagined sinking into Jullian's ass, taking him hard and deep. Setting his empty glass on the counter, he surmised that they had plenty of time to kill.

Jullian turned just as Sebastian reached him. With his hands on his shoulders, Sebastian shoved, forcing Jullian to the wall behind him with a grunt. Desire flared in his friend's eyes as Sebastian leaned closer, covering Jullian's mouth with his own.

* * * * *

Rebecca lounged before the fire, watching the flames lick at the air. The wood crackled and popped, sending a lone spark to land on the rock hearth. She watched as the red ember slowly faded, her mind on the last few hours.

Dinner had been wonderful. The food amazing, the wine delicious, the company entertaining. Tonya had seemed a little distracted but assured her she was fine, just tired. Once they'd finished Marcus had escorted Tonya to the garden, his hand possessive at the small of her back. She was certainly thankful they'd brought her here but at the same time Rebecca wished her friend didn't have to go through this.

She couldn't even begin to imagine what she must be thinking. Her lover a vampire? That would be enough to drive anyone over the edge. Unfortunately they hadn't had an opportunity to talk about it. Hopefully they would have some time alone tomorrow. If she could keep Marcus away from her for a few hours. The man appeared to be permanently attached to the girl's hip.

Her gaze wandered to the door where Nicholas and Darien had just strolled in, shutting it behind them. And speaking of men who appeared to be attached to their women...

"Don't the two of you have something to do?" she drawled, ignoring the tingle of desire running down her spine at the sight of them together.

"Yes," Nicholas purred in a sexy timbre, making goose bumps rise along her flesh. Just the sound of his deep voice could make her pussy wet.

"How were your lessons?" Nicholas asked as he dropped onto the sofa beside her. Darien moved in behind her, his fingers gently massaging her shoulders. It felt wonderful and she slowly began to relax.

"Like you weren't there the whole time," she replied, closing her eyes with a soft moan, allowing Darien's fingers to gently work their relaxing magic.

"I wasn't there the *whole* time."

"But long enough you saw what a botched job I did," she said with a sigh.

"You'll get it," Darien whispered, then placed a soft kiss on her neck.

"Will I really? Aren't I too old for this? Isn't there an age where learning magic becomes harder?"

Nicholas chuckled. "No. You'll get it, Rebecca. I know you will."

The backs of his fingers brushed along her cheek and she turned her head slightly to study his sincere expression. He really did believe she would eventually get it and the very idea he had that much faith in her made her warm all over.

Reaching out, she touched his cheek and smiled at the stubble that scraped her fingers. He turned his head, capturing her fingers in his hand and gently kissing them. A tingle ran up her arm, making her shudder in desire.

His fathomless eyes remained locked on hers as his lips moved to the inside of her wrist, gently nipping at the pulse point. She licked her lips, amazed at the power the two of them had over her. Whether together or separate they could always make her need them beyond reason. She'd been fighting it all day—fighting the memory of that day in the club, fighting her growing physical attraction to them, her need to feel them both inside her, and she swallowed.

"Are you trying to seduce me?" she whispered.

Nicholas' lips twitched in amusement before sensually sliding up the inside of her arm to the sensitive skin at the inside of her elbow. "Maybe. If that's what you want."

Darien moved her hair from the side of her neck and placed a soft kiss just under her ear, making her flesh burn. "Is it what you want, Rebecca?"

She licked her lips, wondering that very thing herself. Her body was screaming yes, her mind and heart still had so many questions. Which should she listen to? Which did she want to listen to?

"Everything is happening so fast," she murmured, her eyes sagging closed. Darien scraped his teeth along the side of her neck, sending sensual chills down her spine.

"It can go as fast or as slow as you want, baby," Nicholas said as he moved to nibble on the other side of her neck. "Do you want us to stop?" he asked, his warm breath blowing across her ear.

She nodded then changed her mind and shook her head. She felt Darien's lips as they spread into a smile against her shoulder. "Which is it? Yes or no?"

Neither man moved as they waited for her answer. She couldn't fight this, she didn't want to fight this. "No. Don't stop."

Turning her head, Nicholas captured her lips in a soul stealing kiss, his tongue invading, twirling and tasting. It left her mindless and drunk from desire. Her whole body hummed with building lust, her pussy leaking cream onto the crotch of her panties. She wanted them off, she wanted to feel their hands all over her body like before. She needed it so much she felt as though she were suffocating from it.

Breaking the kiss, Nicholas moved to settle on his knees between her legs. With a gentle nudge he spread them wide, exposing her aching mound. His fingers moved to the band of her panties and tugged.

"Lift your hips, baby," he commanded softly and she obeyed without thought.

All she could do was feel—her own need as well as theirs. It was the oddest sensation and an overwhelming one at that, as their desire for her screamed through her body to mingle with hers, intensifying it.

"You have such nice legs, Becca," Nicholas whispered as he gently placed one leg over the arm of the couch. "Hmmm," he purred. "And such a nice, wet pussy."

His lips touched the inside of her thigh, making her gasp. Darien remained behind her, his mouth softly toying with her earlobe, his fingers loosening the front buttons of her dress. Slowly Nicholas worked his way higher, ever closer to her already aching mound, and she bit down on her lip to keep from begging him to lick her.

"Is this some kind of magic trick?" she gasped as Nicholas blew against her labia.

"No, sweet," Darien whispered.

He spread open the top of her dress, exposing her bra and heaving breasts. Her nipples were hard and extended even behind the lace covering them. He palmed one, making her groan and arch her back. "You need us as much as we need you. We're one now."

His lips moved to nip a trail down the side of her neck, making her senses jump to life. Nicholas spread her labia, gently licking his tongue along her slit. She moaned, dropping her head back against the cushions. Darien leaned forward, licking across her nipples through the lace, making her shiver in delight.

When Nicholas' tongue flattened against her clit her hips bucked, shoving her pussy into his face. "Oh God," she moaned, now completely on fire from head to toe.

"Mmmm, you taste good," he murmured then continued his leisurely strokes, deliberately avoiding where she wanted him to touch her the most.

Juices poured from her body to coat his face and moisten between the cheeks of her ass. She wanted him so badly she could cry. Sensations slammed through her as she opened herself up to their sensations, their feelings. She could feel the pressure in their balls, the need pounding through their veins, the desire to give her pleasure and it intensified her own, made her almost animalistic to get what she needed.

"Please," she hissed, undulating her hips against Nicholas's mouth.

"On your knees," Nicholas ordered and she sat up, facing him. "Face the other way. Face Darien."

She frowned at first then moved to her knees, facing the back of the couch. Darien moved to sit on the back, his slacks undone, his cock free and thick. He was so gorgeous, his eyes aglow with the same desire eating her alive. She licked her lips as she stared, enraptured by the purple head now glistening with drops of precum. Darien growled then gripped her dress, helping Nicholas to lift it over her head.

Next her bra dropped to the floor, freeing her breasts. Darien stared at her in fascination, his eyes glowing hungrily as they raked over her form, and her stomach jerked at the intensity of his gaze. The warm air of the room washed over her naked form, searing her skin and puckering her nipples. Nicholas thrust two fingers into her wet channel just as Darien leaned forward to nibble at her neck. She cried out, holding tight to Darien's hair. Sex with two men was amazing. It was everything she needed and then some.

Moving her hips in time with Nicholas' fingers, she moaned her pleasure, silently begging them for more. Darien pulled away, his fingers gripping the base of his cock. "Lick me," he whispered.

She leaned forward quickly, hungry for the first taste of his massive cock. She wanted to give him the same pleasure they gave her. Her tongue licked across the head, savoring the salty taste of his cum. Darien groaned his approval, encouraging her to continue. "That's it, baby. Take it in your mouth."

Opening her lips, she engulfed only half of his length. It was all she could fit in her mouth. With her tongue she teased the head, circling the shaft just under it. Nicholas had stopped his thrusts, holding his fingers deep inside her. She knew he watched her. She could sense his gaze, feel his burning lust and it drove her on, made her wild. With little embarrassment she realized she enjoyed the fact that he watched.

His fingers began to move again, slowly at first then harder, more demandingly. She gasped, thrusting her hips back to take them deeper. With a growl of his own he removed his fingers and replaced them with a hard thrust of his huge shaft. She groaned, gently biting down on Darien's cock. He growled, burying his fingers in her hair and tugging her down, forcing more of his cock into her mouth. Relaxing her throat, she took all of him, just like she took all of Nicholas into her pussy. He pounded into her—hard demanding thrusts that just made her hungry for more and she pushed back, using her body to beg for it.

"Damn," Darien growled, his body tightening. "Your mouth feels so good, baby. Can you feel it? Can you feel what your mouth is doing to me?"

She could. In her mind she could feel every swipe of her tongue, every gripping throb of her channel is it held tight to Nicholas. She whimpered around his cock, so close to shattering into a million pieces she could hardly breathe. Of course the cock down her throat wasn't helping matters either but he tasted so good she didn't want to let him go. Nicholas fucked her so hard her pussy burned, clenching at his shaft and sucking it even deeper. She could feel his lust as well, his building release as hers hit.

Their three emotions melted into one blinding orgasm as Darien spurted his seed down her throat and Nicholas came into her pulsing pussy. Over and over it washed through her, around her, almost strangling her with its intensity.

Nicholas moved slowly, gently thrusting in soothing motions as she licked Darien's cock clean. The room spun, her mind clinging precariously to consciousness and she dropped her forehead to Darien's leg, spent and satisfied beyond anything she could imagine. In the back of her mind she imagined she'd felt their love for her but she shoved it aside, unsure she was ready to face that just yet.

Chapter Seven

න

"How are you holding up, Tonya?" Rebecca asked as they followed the stone path through the center of the garden.

"I don't know," she said with a tired sigh. "I still feel like I'm stuck in the middle of some dream."

Rebecca laughed. "Yeah, me too. Wonder if we'll ever wake up?"

"Do you really want to? I mean you've always wanted two men smothering you with attention and sex." Tonya wiggled her eyebrows.

"I'll admit the sex is amazing. More than I ever imagined. I just never dreamed I'd be in the middle of something so wild. Arrogant talking cats, vampires, a Witches Council. What's next? Aliens?"

Tonya snorted then shook her head, making her ponytail swing back and forth. "Let's not give the universe any more ideas. Let me get used to what's here before I have to forget everything I learned as a child."

"I'm glad you're here," Rebecca whispered. "I don't know what I would have done if I didn't have someone to talk to about all this."

"Me too." Tonya smiled and squeezed her hand. "At least you understand some of what I'm going through with Marcus. It's the strangest thing. I can sense him when he's near. Smell him. It's like he's a part of me and the second…well the second I see desire in his eyes I feel it as well. And it's uncontrollable. Undeniable."

"I know. I'm the same way with Darien and Nicholas. They told me that's the way it is with their kind. Once they find their mate it's unstoppable and since Marcus is half warlock it's that way with him as well."

Rebecca stopped to pluck a pink rose from the bushes lining the path. Nudging Tonya's arm, she pointed to the white unicorn grazing in the field close by. It was so beautiful and graceful and didn't appear to be the least bit afraid as it raised its head to stare at them.

"It's beautiful," Tonya whispered.

"I know. I want to touch it but I'm afraid I'll frighten it away."

Tonya grasped her elbow and tugged her back toward the path so they could resume their walk.

"Do you know why this Sebastian wants you dead?" Tonya asked.

"He's the closest relation to my father so if I die the seat reverts to him. Since he can't hold two seats it's up to him to assign it to someone else. Nicholas believes he has a vampire in mind. There are rumors circulating he's been seen with one of the more dangerous vampires, Vlad."

Tonya looked at her with a frown. "I don't understand."

"Don't understand what?" Marcus asked from behind them, making both of them squeal in surprise.

"Don't do that!" Tonya snapped. "God, put a bell around your neck or something. And how did you find us? Did you stick a LoJack in my bra?"

Rebecca laughed. Clamping her hand over her mouth, she stared apologetically toward Marcus. He grinned, showing off that adorable smile and for the first time sporting a five o'clock shadow.

"Gotta love that mouth of hers," he replied with a chuckle. "Now back to the conversation. What is it you don't understand? Maybe I can help."

"What difference does it make if Sebastian gives my seat to a vampire?" Rebecca asked.

"Well." With a frown, Marcus pointed to a bench nestled beneath a shade tree and they made their way over to sit down—Tonya and Rebecca on the ends, Marcus between them. "To be honest, just giving it to a vampire is not that big a deal, considering there're already vampires on the council. Where the problem would arise is if there were more vampires than witches. That would mean the vampires would control the council, which would not bode well for the witches, or the mortal world for that matter."

"Why?" Tonya asked.

"To be honest, vampires and witches have a weak treaty at best. There's always that underlying field of tension. Plus the witches keep a tight rein on the vampires."

"That puts you in an awkward position doesn't it?" Tonya asked. "Being from both worlds?"

"Sometimes," he agreed. "I'm more comfortable with witches. I grew up with them. I met Darien and Nicholas about twelve years ago. We've been friends ever since."

"So if there's more witches than vampires, what would one more vampire do?" Rebecca asked.

Marcus thought for a moment, his brows drawn together in a frown. "Right now if another vampire was added they would be equal, which in itself could cause problems."

"There's got to be more to this," Tonya said with a shake of her head. "Something we don't know."

"That's obvious." Marcus put his hand on Tonya's knee and squeezed. Rebecca didn't miss the flare of heat that sparked in her friend's eyes as she looked up at him. "Now the objective is to find out what it is we're missing."

Rebecca sighed and glanced toward the white clouds floating by. The scents of rose and jasmine mingled with pine, making her think of spring back home. "Why do I have a feeling that's going to be a lot harder than it sounds?"

Marcus chuckled. "Probably because it is."

An image flashed through Rebecca's mind, similar to the image she had in her apartment and others she'd had in the past. The same man she'd seen before but this time he had fangs. Long, distended fangs. She shivered, blinking the image from her mind.

"I know!" Rebecca raised her hands toward the sky in a flash of brilliance and spouted off her idea, based on the image she'd seen in her mind. "Sebastian is a vampire and nobody knows it."

She opened her eyes to find Marcus and Rebecca staring at her as though she'd sprouted three heads. Her grin faded. "What? It was a joke."

Marcus nodded his head then shook it. "Yes, but very plausible." His eyes narrowed as he studied her, making her slightly uncomfortable. "Did you see something, Rebecca?"

"What do you mean?" she asked.

"Your mother had visions. Did you see something or were you just being silly?"

She swallowed, remembering her image. "I saw something."

"What?"

"A vampire. But how can a witch be a vampire?" Rebecca asked.

Marcus waved his hand, a silly grin widening his lips. "Oh yeah," she said with her own grin.

"Sebastian was born a warlock. But he can be bitten by a vampire and turned into one just like anyone else."

"But would he have done that deliberately? Let a vampire turn him?" Tonya appeared to be just as confused as Rebecca.

Rebecca sat up straight, turning to better face Marcus. "And wouldn't you know?"

"Not necessarily. Damn, could it be that simple? Turn himself into a vampire, form an allegiance with the ones on the council, promising them control. Take over. Son of a bitch."

Marcus stood. "I'm going to talk to Nicholas. I'll see you ladies later."

With that he disappeared in a flash of light right before their eyes. Tonya scowled toward the empty spot where he stood just seconds before. "I hate it when he does that."

* * * * *

Nicholas stood in the center of the lab, studying the scroll hanging in mid-air—Vincent's latest version of a protection spell. It was powerful but it had holes. Holes they needed to plug before they could use it. He refused to risk Rebecca. Now that he'd found her he didn't think he could let her go.

"Marcus is coming," Vincent said with a swish of his tail and Nicholas looked to where he nodded to see Marcus appear in a flash of soft blue light.

"Is there a problem?" Nicholas asked.

"Rebecca just blurted out a very plausible idea that needs a little delving into."

"You want to elaborate?" Nicholas asked, intrigued.

"She thinks Sebastian allowed himself to be turned into a vampire so when he appoints a vampire to Rebecca's seat—"

"The vampires will control the council," Vincent finished for him.

"Exactly," Marcus said with a nod.

Nicholas frowned and brushed his hair back over his shoulder. "How do we find out without tipping him off?"

"I'll start with my father. See if he's heard anything."

"Do you know where he is?" Vincent asked, his ear sticking up in interest, his hair standing on end.

Marcus shrugged a shoulder. "He usually spends this time of year in Romania, I'll begin there. It'll be sundown in about an hour. If I use magic I can be back in less than three. Hopefully with a little more information."

86

"If he's been transformed this changes everything," Vincent purred, his head tilting in thought.

"This changes nothing," Nicholas argued. "Vampire or Warlock, the man needs to be exposed and banished."

Vincent hissed, surprising Nicholas. "The man's killed at least two people that we know of. If he has truly transformed into a vampire we cannot banish him to the mortal world. Death is the only option."

* * * * *

Marcus strolled around his father's study, glancing over various pieces of art and two hundred-year-old manuscripts. The man had a fortune in this room alone. He and his father weren't close by any means. Strained was more like it. His father made sure he and his mother had been financially taken care of and for that Marcus would always be grateful but his warlock blood tended to rub his father the wrong way.

More than once Marcus had wondered, if his father disliked witches so much how had he ended up with his mother?

"Marcus?"

The sound of his father's surprised voice pulled him from his trip down memory lane and he turned to look at him. He never aged, never looked a day over thirty-two, which was how old he'd been when he transformed. Marcus had inherited his deep blue eyes and rich black hair, his height and strong Mediterranean features but that's where the resemblance stopped.

"Not that I don't enjoy seeing you but...what are you doing here?"

Marcus raised an eyebrow at his father's unusually nervous demeanor. "Nice to see you too, Jullian. If you're worried I'll find out about the male lover you have upstairs you shouldn't be." Jullian tilted his head to the side, his eyes widening slightly in surprise. "I've known about your pastime for a while now."

"I see," Jullian replied as he strolled into the room and took a seat behind his desk. "What can I say, Marcus? Women had begun to bore me."

Marcus snorted. "Your personal life is your own. No need to explain. I couldn't really care less."

"So why are you here?" Jullian asked, his eyes narrowing into hard, cold slits.

"I've heard a rumor and I want to see if you've heard it as well."

Jullian nodded. Resting his elbows in the desk, he folded his hands before his lips, his brow drawn in thought. "What's the rumor?"

"That Sebastian has been Transformed."

Jullian remained silent for several moments, his eyes guarded and unreadable. "I don't believe I've heard that one."

Marcus shrugged, watching his father closely. Something in his gut told him he'd just been lied to. "Will you do some checking around?"

"Why?" Jullian asked, relaxing back into his brown leather chair.

"Just consider it a favor for me," Marcus replied as he crossed his leg over his thigh, his hand resting on his ankle.

Jullian nodded. "Fine. I'll see what I can find out."

* * * * *

Sebastian stood just on the other side of the door, his anger and anxiety rising with every second that passed. Who had found out? Who'd spread the rumor? Vlad would never hand him over but Marcus could be a problem. He needed to get a handle on him before he convinced enough people to raise doubt and concern within the council.

Stepping away from the door, he waved toward his assistant. The young man had been with him for years and he knew he could trust him. "Yes, sir?" he asked.

"Find Vlad. Tell him I need a favor."

"Yes, sir," his assistant replied with a nod then turned to do his bidding.

It was time to take care of Marcus.

* * * * *

Marcus strolled through the darkening streets of Slatina, his father's hometown. Every twenty years or so Jullian would go somewhere else for a while but he'd always come back to this home. This is where his father had brought him after his mother died, to teach him vampire history and rules. Yes, vampires had rules. Strict rules that, if broken, more often than not resulted in execution.

As much as he appreciated everything Jullian had done for him and his mother, he just didn't fit into his father's world, which had been their biggest problem. Jullian had wanted him to abandon his warlock side and he wouldn't. He couldn't. He felt more at home with his mother's people. Probably because that was where he'd spent his childhood. It's where he'd grown up and become the man he was.

It hadn't taken his father long to realize how he felt. When he did he reluctantly let him go but Marcus hadn't missed his father's disappointment. He'd wanted a son. A son to teach, to hunt with, but Marcus just couldn't be that son. He couldn't be anything other than what he was. A half-breed.

The cool night breeze blew and he pushed his collar up around his neck, warding off the chill and the sudden feeling of uneasiness. Someone followed him.

Making a right, he turned down a side street and faded into the shadows. It would be better to flush them out now than to allow them to follow him back to England. After several seconds of seeing nothing he finally decided it had only been his imagination. Apparently he was trying to find trouble where there wasn't any.

Cautiously, he made his way back to the main street, anxious to get to his hotel room, where he could transport back. He wasn't strong enough to transport that far on his own. He needed the circle Vincent had helped him to set up several years ago. He could be anywhere and use any material, which was great if he needed to do it quickly. It worked like a booster, strengthening his powers. Unfortunately he had to be in the circle before it would work.

His father didn't allow the use of magic in his home and Marcus had always been careful to honor that request. Although right now he could care less about his father's sensibilities.

The hair on the back of his neck stood on end. Straining, he listened carefully but heard nothing. He would swear there was someone behind him.

Turning, he caught a blur of black right before he was hit in the chest, knocked back against the wall with a thud. His head hit the stone and he grunted, blinking his eyes to clear his fading vision and block the pain pounding the back of his neck. What the hell had hit him?

Focusing his gaze, he caught the blur again but this time raised his hands to block the attacker.

"*Manista*," he murmured, using magic to protect himself.

The attacker stopped inches from him as though he'd hit a wall then fell to the ground in a groaning heap. Marcus took a good look at the man on the ground. Long blond hair framed an angelic face and ice blue eyes. Blood-red lips curled back, showing fangs, distended and sharp. Vlad.

"What the hell are you doing, Vlad?" Marcus snapped.

Fast as lightening Vlad rose and slapped Marcus across his cheek with the back of his hand. Bright lights temporary blinded him as he turned and hit the stone wall again, this time scraping his cheek. With a groan he worked his jaw, trying to determine if it was broken.

Vlad's fingers gripped the back of his neck, pinning him between Vlad's chest and the wall. The stone bit into his flesh and a warm trickle of blood slid down his cheek. Vlad inhaled, bringing his nose close to Marcus' flesh.

"Jullian would never allow it, Vlad, and you know it," Marcus hissed.

"I couldn't care less what Jullian would allow, half-breed," Vlad growled. "I should drain your blood now, relieve your father of his half-breed son, his embarrassment."

"Fuck you," Marcus snarled.

Vlad laughed then scraped his fangs across the surface of Marcus's flesh but not deep enough to draw blood.

"Stay away from here, Marcus. Stop asking questions and keep your nose out of it or I'll have no choice but to rid you of your curse."

Marcus frowned. "How did you know I was asking questions?"

Vlad licked his cheek and Marcus growled, his own fangs dropping into place as his anger rose.

"Let's just say a little birdie told me," Vlad whispered.

Closing his eyes, Marcus concentrated hard, trying to focus on the magic and not suspicion that his father might be involved in all this—that his father had sent Vlad to do what he couldn't.

Vlad tensed then screamed as pain sliced through him. He loosened his hold on Marcus and slid to the ground, his body contorting at odd angles. "Stop it," he hissed.

"Who sent you?" Marcus asked, scowling down at the pain-racked vampire. "Was it my father?"

Vlad shook his head but didn't speak. Marcus concentrated, worsening the pain. "Who sent you?" he asked again.

"Sebastian," Vlad gasped.

"Where is he?" Marcus yelled.

Vlad shook his head, barely able to speak. "He's gone. I was just to deliver the message. Make it stop, Marcus. I'm on fire."

"In time," Marcus drawled as he squatted next to Vlad. "You deliver this message for me. Tell him I know what he's up to and he'll gain control of the council over my dead body."

* * * * *

Darien shook his head, staring at the spell as it hung in the air between him and Nicholas. "You realize this is dabbling in the black arts."

"We've done it before," Nicholas murmured with a shrug.

"Just because we got away with it once doesn't mean we should drop our guard and do it again," Darien growled, waving his hand to erase the spell.

Vincent jumped onto the cabinet, rattling the glass jars against one another. Blue smoke lifted from the powder his paws landed smack in the middle of. "Get off your high horse, Darien. It takes black magic to fight black magic."

Darien rested his hands at his hips and shot the cat a glare. "Careful, cat, or I'll drop you off at the nearest farmer's hut where you can live off mice and fresh milk for the rest of your sentence."

Vincent hissed, his eyes narrowing to tiny slits.

"Enough," Nicholas sighed. "Vincent is right, Darien. If we're going to do this we have to use all our options. And that includes black magic."

Darien paced, his chest tightening in fear and apprehension. "So we take her to the ball, parade her around in the hope that Sebastian will see her and do something stupid? Do you realize what kind of risk we're taking with her life?"

Nicholas growled and knocked one of the vials off the cabinet. Yellow liquid spilled across the floor, releasing a strong flower scent into the room. "Don't you think I've thought this through? I'm terrified we'll fail, Darien. I'm terrified we'll lose her but I refuse to spend the rest of our lives in fear of that damn warlock! I want him taken care of so we can go on with our lives!"

"Marcus," Vincent murmured just before a flash of light lit up the room.

Darien turned to stare at Marcus in surprise. A bruise had begun to form on his cheek, his eye swollen and turning black. His usual neat appearance had been replaced with dirt-smudged clothes and rumpled hair.

"What the hell happened to you?" Darien asked.

"Vlad," Marcus snarled and nodded toward Vincent. "What have you got for this mess, Vincent?" he asked, pointing toward his cheek. "I don't want Tonya seeing it."

"I think it's a little late for that." Nicholas nodded toward the doorway.

Marcus turned to face Tonya. Her eyes widened in surprise then concern as she ran forward. "Are you okay?" she asked, gingerly touching his cheek.

"I'm fine, sweet," he whispered, grabbing her hand and placing a kiss on the center of her palm.

Rebecca stood back, her gaze moving from Marcus to the various vials and jars littering the room. "What is this place? A lab?"

"Of sorts," Darien said as he strolled forward and took her hand in his. Her fingers were cold, her gaze full of worry. "You all right?"

She nodded, giving him a soft smile, but her gaze didn't change. "Who's Vlad? Is he the one you were talking about earlier?"

"I was just about to ask the same thing," Tonya said, narrowing her eyes at Marcus.

"Yes," Marcus said with a sigh.

"I take it the two of you don't play well together," Tonya said, making everyone snicker.

Marcus grinned. "You could say that. Seems he didn't like my asking questions about Sebastian."

Darien frowned as the heavy weight of doom settled on his shoulders. "How did he even know you were asking questions?"

"Sebastian," Marcus sneered. "I'd bet every dime I have the son of a bitch was in my father's house."

"Do you think your father is in on it?" Vincent asked.

Marcus shook his head as Nicholas led him to a stool, where he rubbed a salve on his cheek. "I'm not sure. Part of me wants to say yes, the other part—the son—wants to give him the benefit of the doubt."

Darien looked down at Rebecca and felt his heart tear into pieces. He couldn't lose her. Not now. Leaning down, he placed a soft kiss on her temple, inhaling the sweet scent of her hair. She glanced up at him, her gaze questioning. With a smile he brushed her bangs from her eyes.

"Is this a magic thing?" Tonya asked as she stepped forward, studying the salve on Marcus' cheek.

"Yes. Want to take care of it?" Nicholas asked, handing Tonya the small bottle.

Her eyes widened slightly. "Can I?"

"Of course. It's the salve that has the magical properties, not the person applying it."

Tonya took the bottle and sniffed, crinkling her nose in distaste. "This is disgusting."

Darien shared a grin with Marcus.

"We'll take it to the garden," Marcus offered, putting his hand at the base of Tonya's spine and leading her to the door. "I'll get with you guys later about Sebastian."

Darien nodded.

"I'll meet you on the veranda for breakfast, Tonya," Rebecca said and Tonya waved her consent, making Rebecca grin. "She's so crazy about him. She just doesn't realize it yet." Her gaze wandered around the shelves, her fingers turning bottles so she could read the labels. "What is all this stuff?" she asked in curiosity.

"Herbs mostly," Vincent replied. "Some of them are pretty powerful, so be careful."

"Why?" she asked with a cheeky grin as she lifted a bottle from one of the higher shelves. "Will it blow me up?"

Removing the cork, she lifted the bottle to her nose. Darien noticed the label and gasped, trying to stop her before she inhaled too much. "Rebecca, no!"

It was too late. She inhaled a huge whiff then gasped, her eyes widening and filling with unshed tears. "Oh my god. What is this?"

Vincent snickered. "Better get her to bed quick. She took in a good bit of that."

Nicholas cursed and grabbed Rebecca's waist just as her knees gave way. "Whoa, sweetheart."

She giggled, waving her hand dismissively. "I'm not a hor...horse," she said with a hiccup.

"No, you're definitely not a horse, but you're one fucked-up witch," Darien murmured with barely contained humor.

"I haven't been fucked up yet," she purred, making Darien's cock harden. "Am I drunk?"

He caught his brother's raised eyebrow over her head and almost laughed at his strained expression. She'd taken a huge sniff of the magical herb, enough that the effects would probably last for hours.

"Sort of," Darien replied.

With another drunken giggle, she turned to grasp Nicholas' shirt in her fingers. "Come on, Nicky. Fuck me up. Fuck me up really good, like last time."

Nicholas' lips twitched as Darien stepped forward and tugged at her tiny wrist, pulling her away from his brother. "Come on, sweet. Let's take this upstairs."

"Oh yes," she sighed, her words slurred adorably. "I like it when you both take me, when you both give me..." She hiccuped, making Nicholas chuckle. "When you both give me... What were we talking about again?" she asked, her brow drawn in the most adorable frown.

She tripped over something on the floor, laughing as she attempted to right herself. Nicholas moved forward and took her other arm, wrapping her hand around his elbow.

"You should learn to ask before you sniff, Becca," Nicholas said with a grin. "You never know what you'll end up with."

"Did I sniff something?" She smiled. "I think you would look good with a white streak like Darien."

"Then you wouldn't be able to tell us apart."

"Sure I would," she replied proudly. "You call me baby and Darien calls me sweet."

Nicholas and Darien laughed as they came to a stop at the bottom of the stairs. Bending, Darien lifted her in his arms. With a squeal, she wrapped her arms around his neck, holding tight.

"Oh, you're so strong," she murmured, burying her face in his neck.

Her breath felt warm against his skin. Her body curled against his chest perfectly, like she belonged there. And she did. Drunk on a magical herb or not, he wanted to take her upstairs and make love to her for as long as she could take it. Glancing at Nicholas, he noticed the same deepening desire in his gaze as well. Damn, they were so screwed.

Her lips nibbled along the column of this throat, sending prickles of heat straight to his balls. "You're drunk, sweet," he whispered.

"I'm not that drunk," she purred, licking her tongue along his jawline.

"Yes you are, baby," Nicholas said with a soft chuckle. "You won't remember any of this tomorrow."

"Nothing?" she murmured, running her hand through Darien's hair.

"Not a thing," Darien agreed as they reached their bedroom door. "But I certainly will and you're going to pay for this."

Opening it, he slipped through while Nicholas followed and closed it behind him. Rebecca continued to kiss along his neck, driving him crazy. Her lips were warm, her fingers soft as they slipped inside his shirt and feathered along his chest. He glanced over his shoulder at his brother, who watched the whole scene with amusement.

"She's killing me," Darien hissed. "Don't just stand there. Do something."

Nicholas shrugged. "Like what?"

"Like screwing me," Rebecca whispered, flicking her thumb across his nipple in a way that made his knees weak.

This was insane. He refused to fuck her in this condition. She wouldn't remember any of it and would probably be pissed as hell if she found out they'd taken advantage of her.

"I'm so turned on my pussy actually hurts. It needs you, Nicky," she murmured and Darien sighed.

"It's Darien, sweet."

"My ass needs you, Darien."

Darien swallowed and glared at his brother across the top of her head. "Help me get her to bed before I give her what's she's begging for."

Nicholas swallowed and moved forward, throwing back the covers. Darien laid her in the center, untangling her fingers from his hair. She moaned, arching her back enticingly and he swallowed down his lust. He needed to get control of himself.

His brother wasn't much better off if the hard-on outlined behind his jeans was any indication.

Her hands moved to cup her breasts, squeezing them with her fingers through the material of her top. His cock twitched as he watched her—eyes closed, lips open and moist. God, tempting didn't even begin to cover how she looked.

"Take them off," she begged. "Take off my clothes, please. I'm so hot."

"I wish she would hurry the hell up and pass out," Darien snarled.

Nicholas chuckled, using trembling fingers to undo the button of her slacks. "You and me both," he sighed, tugging at her pants.

"Oh yes," she hissed, lifting her hips as he pushed her pants over her bottom.

Darien inhaled, catching the scent of her arousal. She smelled heavenly, like honey and musk. Nicholas dropped her pants to the floor while Darien worked on her top. *Think of anything else but the sight of those luscious globes, all swollen and firm, her rosy nipples round and erect.*

With a groan she sat up suddenly, tugged her own top off and threw it across the room with impatience. Her bra was next, landing on the dresser a few feet away. "Oh that feels so much better." Dropping to her back, she stretched, smiling coyly up at Nicholas. "Come on, Nicholas. Lick them."

His brother looked at him, his brows drawn tight from the strain of holding back.

"Please, one of you, give me some relief," she begged, her words even more slurred now than before.

The drug was taking a deeper hold and she'd soon be sound asleep. Would it hurt to give her a little relief before she passed out? Leaning down, Darien licked his tongue across one engorged nipple. She gasped, arching her back and shoving her breasts further into his mouth. Nicholas slid her underwear off then used his palms to spread her legs.

Her scent wafted up to surround him, intensifying his need to bury his cock inside her. He and Nicholas both slid their hands between her legs, stroking her labia through the thick juices coating her. Together he and Nicholas slid a finger inside, stroking her tight, hot walls. She moaned in pleasure, her hips undulating along with their slow thrusts, sucking their fingers deeper into her tight passage.

Closing his eyes, Nicholas imagined it was his cock encased in her pussy—imagined it was his cock that her walls squeezed so hungrily. "Feel good, sweet?" he murmured against her lips.

She only whimpered in response, her release close. With a shout she came, her pussy pulsing around their fingers, her cries and scent surrounding them. As quick as it had come she was out like a light, her chest rising and falling with the slow breaths of sleep.

"There's no way in hell I can leave this room," Nicholas whispered. "I can't fucking walk."

Darien laughed, dropping his forehead to the pillow next to Rebecca's head. "Neither can I. We might as well turn in too. It's late anyway."

Nicholas nodded then stripped and climbed into the bed next to Rebecca. Darien followed, wrapping Rebecca in his arms from the other side, her body warm and soft against his.

This was going to be a long night.

* * * * *

Tonya took the handkerchief Marcus handed her and wiped the salve from his cheek. The bruise had faded, leaving healthy tanned skin in its place. She brushed her finger across the healed spot, watching his long lashes flutter against his cheek as he blinked. Just touching him, whether sexually or not, made her stomach flip.

He sat on a bench, his body facing forward as she stood next to him wiping away the last traces of the magical salve.

How did she feel about falling in love with a vampire? How would she feel about giving herself to him fully—biting him so he could make her what he was? How would she feel if she didn't and had to let him go?

His lips lifted in a slight smile as he studied her. "Your eyes give you away," he whispered.

"How so?" she asked, brushing the back of her fingers along his jawline. "What do you see?"

He turned to face her more fully and stared deep into her eyes. She watched the moonlight reflect in the deep blue of his gaze and wondered how she would ever go on without him.

"I see confusion, worry." His lips spread into a sensual grin. "Desire."

She returned his grin as his arm rose to wrap around her waist and pull her close. He buried his face between her breasts, inhaling her scent as he hugged her tight. "I don't want you to ever be afraid of me," he sighed.

With a frown, she ran her fingers through the hair on the top of his head. "I'm not afraid of you. At least not now."

He tilted his head back, staring up at her with eyes full of hunger and her whole body shivered in response, her own hunger rising a notch. She'd never met anyone who could make her feel like this—who could make her weak with passion.

"I want you," he whispered and she ran the tip of her finger down his nose. "I want all of you, Tonya. Forever."

She froze, swallowing the sudden lump in her throat. Could she give him forever? Could she cross over and become something else?

"I—" she began, taking a deep shuttering breath.

"It's okay," he said, interrupting her. "I want you to be sure. When you're ready I'll be here."

Licking at her lips, she felt the heat of a blush move over her face and neck. "Can we still make love?"

He smiled, making her heart skip a beat. "You bet we can, gorgeous."

Grabbing her hands, he tugged, pulling her down to the grass with him. With a laugh she wrapped her arms around his neck and welcomed his lips against hers. She moaned, opening her mouth to accept his kiss. He tasted of warm cider and smelled of hot, aroused male. The desire she felt when he touched her was incredible. Undeniable. He'd hardly touched her and already she wanted him so bad her whole body ached.

His lips moved from hers to blaze a trail down the side of her neck. Strong fingers tugged her top from the waistband of her jeans, exposing the sensitive skin of her stomach. Lifting slightly, she allowed him to remove her top completely. The cool night air brushed across her flesh, making her shiver but the heat in his gaze turned her shivers of cold into shivers of delight.

Her nipples beaded against the lace of her bra as his fingers gently skimmed along the edge, teasing her breasts. With a gentle tug he freed one breast, the heavy mound spilling over to beg for his touch. His tongue flicked across the swollen nipple, making her gasp and arch her back for more.

He was entirely too content to tease and with an aggravated shove she pushed him to his back. Wide blue eyes stared up at her in a mixture of shock, arousal and, surprisingly, love. She stopped, her hands behind her to unclasp her bra and stared into his gaze, the words "I love you" on the tip of her tongue.

"Say it," he whispered.

Swallowing, she unhooked her bra, letting it fall to the ground. His hungry gaze dropped to her breasts and he licked his lips before moving his eyes back to her.

"Say it," he whispered again.

"I think I love you," she sighed, leaning back slightly to undo his pants.

His cock, thick and long, sprang free and she traced her finger down his velvety shaft.

"Just think?" he growled and her lips twitched playfully.

"Just think," she purred then bent over to lick along his length, making him growl.

In a move so fast it shocked her he sat up, grasping her face between his hands and pulling her close. His eyes glowed and his nostrils flared, making her belly tense in need. "Make sure you're certain before you say it because the second you do you're mine. Forever."

Her gasp was swallowed by his kiss as his mouth descended onto hers with almost brutal pressure. His tongue invaded, stealing her very breath as he deepened the kiss, dominated her and left no doubt she was his.

Laying her on the ground, he kissed a path down her stomach. Her hips lifted as his hands slid her jeans over her hips then down her legs. Next came her underwear and she hissed as the night wind blew across her aching pussy.

Marcus spread her legs wide, his lips placing soft nibbling kisses against the inside of her thigh as he slowly worked his way up to her wet mound. Her breaths came out as short pants as her hips lifted off the ground, silently begging him to taste her, to fuck her with his tongue.

His hand rested against her lower stomach, applying just a little pressure. "Be still,"

Tonya bit her lower lip, concentrating hard on keeping her body still. Marcus separated her labia and blew softly against her clit. She moaned, thrashing her head from side to side. She was on fire, every part of her, and if he didn't do something soon she'd combust.

"Marcus, please," she gasped as he slowly licked his tongue along her slit, the tip gently circling her swollen clit.

"But you look so adorable," he purred then rose to flick his tongue across her nipple, making her groan. With his finger, he moved the lace covering her other breast, exposing it to his gaze. "With these gorgeous breasts hanging out, the bit of fabric underneath pressing them upward so that they're just perfect for kissing."

"And these long legs," he purred as his hands skimmed down her thighs. "So perfect."

She moaned, lifting her hips slightly as his fingers moved close to the inside of her thigh. "And this pussy," he whispered, his lips spreading into a sexy grin. "Such a delectable treat."

"Marcus," she groaned.

"Do you want me to touch you there?" he teased, his fingers barely brushing across her labia, making her shudder.

"Yes," she hissed, her hips bucking, blindly searching for his touch.

"How bad?" he teased, his fingers gently stroking her between the globes of her ass.

One finger pressed into the tight hole of her anus, making her jerk in surprise. But a good surprise, she realized once the initial discomfort passed. Juices poured from her pussy to slide down the crevice, lubricating his fingers.

"Oh god," she whimpered as he slowly fucked her ass with his finger.

"Do you want me to lick it?" he whispered in her ear, making her whole body tremble.

She nodded, unable to speak past the lump of need in her throat.

He moved between her legs, his tongue working a slow path along her drenched slit. "Mmmm," he hummed. "So good."

He added a second finger to her ass just as his tongue delved deep into her pussy. Her hips lifted from the ground to grind into his face. Marcus murmured his approval as he continued to lap up her cream, lick away every drop that dripped forth.

Tonya was so close every muscle in her body shook with the intensity of her oncoming release. Marcus' tongue flattened against her clit and she exploded, her body erupting into a mass of heat and sensation. Before she could even begin to relax Marcus slid his fingers from her ass and moved over her. Settling his cock between her legs, he entered her pussy balls-deep with one powerful thrust.

With a loud scream Tonya came again, this one even stronger than the last—every pulse of her pussy pulling him deeper as he pounded into her. Her legs lifted to encircle his hips and he growled, pounding into her with enough force to move her across the grass.

"Fuck," Marcus groaned, hissing and baring his fangs toward the night sky.

Her heart pounded faster as the desire for him to bite her became overwhelming. She needed him to. Needed him to drink from her, make her a part of him.

"Marcus," she whimpered, the stirrings of a third orgasm building in her womb. "Do it. Bite me."

He stared down at her in surprise, his thrusts slowing, his nostrils flaring. She nodded then tilted her head to the side, her body so close to another mind-numbing release she could hardly breathe.

Leaning down, Marcus licked the side of her neck then sank his teeth into her flesh. The sting initially made her gasp but then intensified the pleasure, sending her soaring. She cried out, bucking her hips beneath him as he let go of her neck and shouted toward the night sky, his seed emptying into her greedy pussy.

Chapter Eight

Rebecca stretched along the soft sheets, smiling as her body brushed against the two warm males on either side of her. The morning sun streamed through the open French doors as it rose over the mountain behind them and warmed the wood floors. As she shifted, trying to find a more comfortable position, she frowned, unable to remember how she'd gotten here.

Nicholas turned so that he faced her. His hand rested possessively on her hip, burning her flesh with his touch. "Good morning, my drunken minx," he murmured, his lips twitching slightly.

"Drunken minx?" she murmured. "I don't remember drinking anything."

Darien moved behind her so his chest rested against her back, his legs curled behind hers. "Do you remember sniffing an herb in the lab?" he asked.

She frowned, pursing her lips. She remembered opening a bottle and the overwhelming smell of wood smoke but other than that nothing. "What was that stuff?" she asked, trying to ignore Darien's soft lips as they nibbled along the back of her shoulder.

"It's an herb used to induce intoxication," Nicholas replied, running his finger along her collarbone. "And you took in a lot of it."

Every inch of her skin tingled as they moved closer, sandwiching her between them. It felt so right being here like this. With a hand behind her thigh, Nicholas lifted her leg and settled it over his hip. Juices poured from her pussy to coat the inside of her other thigh and she wiggled, wanting to get closer to his cock as it pressed into her stomach. Darien's cock pressed into her hip, making her gasp with growing desire that snaked along her limbs, warming her from the inside out.

God, how could they do this to her so fast?

"You have no idea what you did to us last night," Nicholas murmured.

Rebecca whimpered, parting her lips as his breath blew across her mouth. She wanted him to kiss her, to feel his tongue dominate her, to taste him. She needed it as much as she needed her next breath of air. Whenever they touched her it was as though she had no control over her body anymore. All she could do was ride the wave of need that enveloped her like a magic spell.

"What did I do to you?" she whispered, licking her tongue across his lower lip.

Darien bit down on her earlobe, making her shiver with delight. "How about we show you," he breathed in her ear.

His hand moved lower, over the rise of her hip then dipped between her legs from behind. She sighed, arching her back slightly and thrusting her hips toward his fingers as they separated her wet labia with featherlike strokes. Every part of her burned with a need she couldn't control. Right now she didn't know if she even wanted to control it. She knew they could give her unbelievable pleasure so she'd given up the fight— choosing to feel as opposed to trying to think it to death.

Their skill in the bedroom had won her body but their understanding, patience and adorable senses of humor had begun to win her heart.

Nicholas nibbled along her neck, sending sparks of heat straight to her core. Darien continued with the teasing strokes, deliberately driving her mad. Her fingers feathered along Nicholas' chest, following the rise and fall of his muscles as she worked her way lower over the ridges of his abs. Her hand gently wrapped around his thick shaft, squeezing as she stroked upward. The thin covering of skin felt like velvet as she worked her way to the tip.

His hips jerked forward as he moaned his approval. Warm fingers came up to pluck at her nipples. Pain mingled with pleasure to send her soaring higher, increasing her need for them. Even their smells drove her wild. Hot, musky male mixed with a little spice. It was heaven.

Darien slipped two fingers into her dripping pussy from behind and she gasped, whimpering for more as he stretched her tight passage. Moving from her pussy, he slid his wet fingers into her ass, gently at first, stretching her with scissorlike motions. Nicholas added his fingers to her pussy, almost sending her into immediate orgasm.

"Shhh," Darien purred, slowing his thrusts to match Nicholas'. "Not yet. I want to be inside you when you come."

"Then you better hurry," she groaned, panting to keep herself under control. She was so close she could taste it but they kept what she needed from her, they deliberately kept her on that edge.

When Nicholas removed his fingers she whimpered in protest but he covered her mouth with his, silencing her cries as Darien thrust into her pussy from behind, filling her to the womb.

"Like that, baby?" he purred.

She moaned, her fingers digging into Nicholas' hip.

Darien pulled out, allowing Nicholas to enter her from the front. She ground her hips against him, loving the sensation of the opposing strokes—one from the back then another from the front. They switched again, neither missing a beat as they continued to torment her from both positions. But she needed more.

"Please," she sighed. "Oh please, I need more. I need you both."

They shifted slightly, Nicholas pulling out of her pussy and allowing Darien to position himself at the tight rosebud opening of her anus. She tensed, her body so wild with need she could hardly breathe. Darien pushed gently but she wanted none of that and shoved against him, pushing half his cock in her ass before he could stop himself.

She cried out, clenching her fingers into Nicholas' hip to pull him closer, to pull him inside her as well. She wanted to feel them together as one. She needed the both of them at once. It made her feel whole, a part of them. With a groan he answered her need, thrusting his cock inside her aching passage. She gulped in huge amounts of air as both Nicholas and Darien shoved forward, filling her impossibly deep, giving her all they had.

Darien cursed and buried his face in her neck, his nails digging into her waist as he held himself still. Nicholas remained still as well, the muscles of his neck and chest tensed and corded.

"She's so damn tight," Darien hissed, slowly pulling out to push back in and seat himself even deeper.

The fullness was breathtaking, almost overwhelming as they both slowly began to move in counterpoint, Nicholas pushing in as Darien pulled out. But only at first. Once her body became accustomed to the torturous pleasure and pain they began to move together, both thrusting deep with perfect timing that quickly sent her into orbit.

Her whole body tensed and shivered with her oncoming release. It built from her core, moving outward like a wave, and she screamed, holding nothing back as her body shattered into a million pieces. She could feel them, feel their pleasure as her pussy and ass spasmed around their cocks, milking them, draining them of everything they had.

Both men groaned as they increased their thrusts, pounding into her so hard she thought they might break her in two. Surprisingly, she came again, splintering into a million tiny pieces of shuddering sensation. With a shout they came, spilling their seed deep inside her. She fought to hold onto consciousness as their orgasms swam through her, mingling with her own.

Darien placed soft kisses along the back of her shoulder while Nicholas rained them across her brow. Every part of her was as limp as a rag doll, sated and spent. She couldn't move much less speak. All she could do was moan and let their hands and lips soothe her.

"God, making love with you is incredible," Nicholas sighed, his lips moving against hers with his words.

She smiled slightly, the words "making love" sending a little thrill through her to wrap around her heart. "Like the two of you haven't shared before."

"Not like that," Darien drawled, his breath teasing her ear as he spoke. "I could make love to you all day."

"We have so much to do," she sighed. "So much you have to teach me."

Nicholas placed soft butterfly kisses along her jawline, making her sigh.

"We have four days before the ball. Plenty of time to get your magic into shape and those protection spells in place," Darien whispered.

Her body tensed as she imagined Sebastian getting his hands on her. Would she be strong enough to fight him? Using her to flush him out was a risky plan, she'd known that up-front but had agreed to go along. She wanted her life back. Not necessarily the old one but a life where she could go out, have dinner, see a movie, go shopping. She wanted more mornings like this, more nights sleeping between her warlocks.

Did she love them?

Pulling away slightly, she studied Nicholas' deep blue eyes, his full, gentle lips. Turning to look over her shoulder, she studied Darien. He was a mirror image of Nicholas right down to the cleft in his chin. Except, she thought with a grin, his white streak. Lifting her hand, she pulled at one of the white strands.

"You okay, sweet?" Darien asked, his brows drawn in concern.

One corner of her lips lifted in a wry smile. "I'm fine. Just thinking."

"About what?" Nicholas asked as he gripped her chin, turning her to face him.

"Can't read my mind?" she teased.

He brushed the back of his fingers down her cheek. "You were blocking us."

She frowned. "I was?"

Nicholas nodded with a grin. "Apparently you learn fast."

"I didn't even realize I was doing it."

"Concentrate, Becca," Darien whispered. "What am I thinking?"

She turned her cheek slightly, allowing him to brush his lips across her flesh and she shivered, realizing they were both still buried inside her. "How can I think when you're doing that?"

"You're not concentrating," he purred then slapped her hip with his hand.

The sting startled her and sent tingles down her spine but she did as he requested and tried to concentrate. Closing her eyes, she blocked out the feel of their cocks, partially hard inside her, the feel of their warm bodies surrounding hers.

Pieces of emotions skimmed through her—confusion, worry, desire...love. She opened her eyes and stared at Nicholas. A lot of what she felt from him was mirrored in his gaze as he watched her but there was something more. Words began to form, whispered words.

Hungry...sunshine...kiss me.

"Which one of you wants me to kiss you?" she asked.

Darien chuckled. "Close," he said. "We were suggesting breakfast."

110

"How did I get kiss me from breakfast?" she sighed. "I'm never going to get this."

"Yes you will," Nicholas said with a grin. "Are you hungry?"

Her stomach growled at the mention of food and she grimaced. "It appears that way." Wiggling her hips, she moaned as they pressed forward, filling her again. "But I invited Tonya to breakfast this morning, remember? I told her we'd meet on the veranda."

"I remember," Darien murmured as his hand came around to cup her breasts and toy with her nipple. "But if you keep that up you'll be late."

"It's still early yet," she sighed, her lips lifting in a sexy grin. Nicholas smiled in return, his eyes glowing with the same desire swimming through her own veins.

"Yes it is," Darien teased. "But I think we should take a shower then trade places. It's time I got a taste of that pussy."

* * * * *

"Good morning," Rebecca sang as she dropped into the chair across from Tonya. With a grimace she shifted, taking her weight off her sore ass.

Tonya watched, her lips twitching slightly in amusement but confusion clouded her eyes. "Still like the whole two man aspect?"

The heat of a blush moved over Rebecca's cheeks. "Yeah, for the most part."

Lifting her cup, she sipped at the hot coffee, almost sighing at the warm caramel flavor. She loved caramel. The morning sun had already warmed the veranda and dried the dew covering the flowers. A white unicorn grazed just a few feet away, his gaze silently watching.

"How are you?" Rebecca asked, studying her friend closely.

A breeze blew, ruffling her dark blonde hair and the collar of her green blouse. Her eyelids lowered, shuttering her eyes from view but Rebecca knew that deep inside something troubled her friend.

"I think I'm in love with him," Tonya whispered.

"Tonya, he's immortal."

"I know." Tonya lifted her gaze and stared pleadingly into Rebecca's. "I don't know what to do. He's offered to make me like him so we can be together but I'm terrified. He's only half vampire. What if I turn into a full one?"

"Nicholas told me he can only transform you into what he is. He's half therefore he can only make you half."

With a sigh, Tonya lifted her glass of orange juice then set it back down untouched. "I don't know. What if they're wrong? I want to be with him. I want to..." A single tear slipped down her cheek and Rebecca's heart broke for her. "I just want to be with him."

Reaching across the table, Rebecca put her hand over her friend's trembling one. Her fingers were cold, shaking. "Then do it," Rebecca whispered.

"Do you love them?" Tonya asked and for a second Rebecca wasn't sure what to say.

Did she? She felt something. She knew they felt something but was it love?

"The jury is still out on that," Rebecca replied with a shrug of her shoulder and a cheeky grin meant to distract.

"Rebecca," Tonya coaxed. "I'm your friend, you know. The one you tell everything to. What are you afraid of?"

Sitting up, Rebecca licked her lips and reached for her coffee cup. She tried to pull her thoughts together while she swallowed the warm drink. "That somehow it's not real."

"Honey," Tonya began. "You have to trust your own feelings more."

Rebecca snorted. "Look who's talking."

"I know. I'm just as bad. But in my case I'm considering becoming a vampire. You on the other hand…"

"I, on the other hand, am falling in love with two men who are everything I ever wanted. But how do I know they feel the same way about me? How do I know it's real and not magic? How do I know they're not just fulfilling a duty for their father by protecting me from Sebastian? My god, Tonya. When this is all over I'll be a member of the Witches Council. I'll be a part of the ruling body that governs this…" she waved her hand, "other world. I don't have a clue what I'm doing. I can't even perform magic beyond the parlor tricks we did as kids. I'm nowhere near Darien's and Nicholas' capabilities and we only have a few days left to get me there. What if I fail?"

This time it was Tonya's turn to learn forward and offer comfort. "You may not have any but I have faith in you. I know you can do this."

* * * * *

Rebecca stood back, concentrating hard on the bird flying toward her. Raising her hand, she spoke softly. "*Vilat.*"

The bird stopped, hovering in mid-air, its wings frozen in flight. Slowly, she walked around it, amazement making her smile. She'd frozen the bird in time.

"You did it," Tonya squealed and the bird's wings flapped, returning it to the world of movement. Raising her hands, she covered her mouth. "I'm sorry," she murmured.

Nicholas laughed from his spot on the log behind them. "It's okay, Tonya. It wasn't you. The spell is only temporary."

Rebecca smiled. Her confidence in her magic was growing but she still had so much to learn. Her gaze wandered down Nicholas' muscular form as he walked toward her. Just looking at him made her body tingle. Her physical reaction was part of the reason she felt so insecure in her feelings toward them.

Darien came out of nowhere, his appearance preceded by a dim flash of blue light, and leaned against the side of the large oak tree centered in the middle of the garden. The breeze whipped at his hair, blowing it around his wide shoulders. His arms crossed over his hard chest, his lips spread into a charming smile and her stomach flipped wildly.

"How's it coming?" he asked.

"Slow," Rebecca sighed. "But I did stop the bird."

"You have to remember concentration is the key. Even if you're scared or confused, concentration is the most important element," Nicholas offered and Darien nodded, agreeing with him.

"He's right."

"So what's next on the agenda?" Rebecca asked.

"Lunch," Marcus shouted, making them laugh. "Then it's a shopping trip."

"Shopping?" Rebecca said in surprise. "I didn't think we were able to leave the castle."

"Who said anything about leaving the castle?" Nicholas drawled with a mischievous grin.

"What do you plan on doing? Bringing the shops here?" Tonya asked.

Marcus chuckled and leaned down to kiss her cheek. "And you say you don't have any magic in you."

"You can't be serious," Rebecca cried in shock.

"In a way that's exactly what we're doing. All you and Tonya will have to do is picture in your mind the dress you want and it will appear."

"Every woman's dream shopping spree," Darien teased with a wink.

Rebecca spread her arms out and frowned. "But how do I know what kind of dress to imagine?"

"We can show you images from last year so you have an idea. Of course the color of the clothes is strictly black," Darien said.

"Naturally," Rebecca drawled, making Tonya giggle.

* * * * *

Sebastian paced, glaring angrily at Vlad. "I told you to watch him, Vlad. He's a fucking warlock."

"I know what the hell he is," Vlad hissed. "Does Jullian have any idea what you're up to?"

"Of course not," Sebastian snapped. "He doesn't hold a seat but he supports the council. He wants there to be peace between vampires and witches. If you can imagine it, he likes things the way they are with the mortal world. Vampires live in relative peace and mortals live in ignorance, believing our existence to be a fairytale. Right now I just need his protection. He's a powerful son of a bitch. Both in bed and out," Sebastian added as he picked at his teeth with a toothpick.

Vlad snarled, his eyes narrowing into disgusted slits. "Spare me."

"Like you haven't dabbled in homosexuality," Sebastian sneered.

"Most vampires have, Sebastian. Comes from being bored, but I would prefer to not hear about it, thank you."

Sebastian snorted. "Did you bring me a piece of the circle?"

"Yes." Leaning forward, he dropped the small vial of dust on the desk. "Will this tell you where he went?"

Picking it up, Sebastian studied the vial. "It should."

"Are you going after her yourself?" Vlad asked.

"Of course not. I can't risk going in there." His lips lifted in a sadistic grin. "I'm sending the demons. They're the only ones who can break through the protection spell surrounding her."

"Her who, Sebastian?"

Sebastian glanced up in surprise at Jullian. He reclined in the doorway, his relaxed demeanor a front. Sebastian knew him well enough to know something had pissed him off.

"Jullian. I didn't know you were back."

"Obviously," he drawled, nodding his head toward Vlad but never taking his gaze off Sebastian. "Vlad. Do you mind leaving Sebastian and me alone?"

"Of course not."

Jullian moved to the side but as Vlad passed snarled menacingly, "I would suggest you not go far. You're next."

Vlad visibly swallowed as he left the room. Jullian shut the door with a slam, turning to glare angrily at Sebastian. "What are you up to, Sebastian?" he snarled.

"I'm not up to any more than I've been up to. Just taking care of a little problem that's been plaguing me for a while now. Nothing to concern yourself with."

"Demons are certainly something to concern myself with. You will not have them in my house, Sebastian."

"Of course not," Sebastian drawled.

Standing, Sebastian walked toward him. Jullian dominated the small room, his anger obvious in his tension-filled shoulders, his creased brow and glowing eyes. Sebastian needed to distract him, needed to get his mind off the demons and the conversation he'd overheard.

Sebastian moved behind him and gently ran his fingers through his long black hair. Jullian immediately tensed and Sebastian stilled, instinctively knowing his friend wouldn't be placated so easily.

"Get your hands off me, Sebastian."

With a nod Sebastian stepped aside, studying Jullian's profile as he stared out the window toward the night sky. "Stay away from my son."

Sebastian's eyes widened slightly. "Excuse me?"

"I know Vlad attacked him."

"How do you—?"

Jullian rounded on him, making Sebastian take a step back in apprehension. "It doesn't matter how!"

"He's a half-breed, Jullian. The son of a witch. What does it matter to you?"

"Make no mistake, it matters. He's Kayla's son. My son. I don't know what you're up to and to be honest I don't really care but you will not harm my son, is that clear?"

Sebastian raised his chin, narrowing his eyes in anger toward the dominant vampire.

"Is that clear, Sebastian?" he snapped.

"Crystal, Jullian," Sebastian snarled, glaring at his friend as he left the room, leaving him alone in the dark.

Chapter Nine

ဆ

"What is this?" Rebecca asked as she studied the small circle in the middle of the floor.

"I wanted you to learn how to do this," Nicholas said as he handed her a jar full of gray dust. "This is what they call a capture circle. You say the name of the person you want to go to and it will capture where they are, then send you there."

"Like a portal?"

"Sort of. It's a booster of sorts. It works off your own abilities. The more powerful you are the further you can transport."

She shook her head with a frown. "But I won't always have this with me," she said, indicating the jar in her hand.

"It's not what the circle is made of but the spell."

"Oh," she replied, intrigued. "So I can make it out of anything."

"Yes," Nicholas said, smiling softly.

"So how do I do this? Just make a circle?"

Taking her hand in his, he pulled her further into the center of the dark lab. Moving behind her, he grasped the hand holding the jar.

"First," he whispered in her ear, sending tingles down her spine. "You sprinkle it around you in a circle. Like this." The two of them moved slowly, sprinkling the dust around them. "As you do, you recite the word, *borlasie.*"

"*Borlasie,*" she repeated breathlessly, her mind more on the heat rising in her flesh than the circle.

"Concentrate," he purred, his tone full of amusement.

His lips touched the side of her neck, making her gasp softly. How the hell was she supposed to concentrate with him doing that? "Do I...um...say it more than once?" she asked, trying to ignore his tongue as it flicked out to lick the sensitive spot behind her ear.

"You recite it repeatedly until the circle is closed," he whispered, his fingers moving under her shirt to skim along her flesh.

With a sigh she laid her head back against his chest, enjoying the tenderness of his touch. "I thought we were supposed to be working on magic."

"We are," he murmured. "I'm trying to teach you how to concentrate amid distraction."

"You're definitely distracting."

He chuckled and softly bit her earlobe, making her yelp.

"Magic lessons mixed with sex, hmmm. Wish I'd thought of that," Vincent purred as he jumped onto the counter, his collar sparkling under the soft lights.

Nicholas sighed, his body going tense. "Don't you have a mouse or something you need to catch? I'm sure the castle is full of them."

Vincent licked his lips. "Not anymore."

"Oh that's so gross," Rebecca grumbled.

"Besides, Darien, Marcus and Tonya are waiting for you in the second level salon. Dress shopping, remember?"

"I completely forgot," Rebecca sighed and smiled coyly at Nicholas. "We can always resume this later."

Nicholas tipped up her chin with his finger. "We'll definitely resume this later."

His lips brushed across hers, sending small shivers down her spine, and warmth spread through her belly. Grasping her hand, he scowled over his shoulder toward Vincent. "Come on, cat."

Vincent hissed as he jumped to the floor, his tail flicking at their legs as he passed to run ahead of them. Rebecca giggled at his disdainful attitude. "Has Vincent always been so…?"

"Haughty? Arrogant?" Nicholas asked, glancing down at the cat as he strolled before them, his tale swishing in the air. "He was that way *before* his sentence."

Vincent glanced back, his eyes narrowing into tiny slits. "Careful, warlock, or you'll find your clothes shredded come morning."

Rebecca snickered then slapped her hand over her mouth. Once she'd gotten used to the idea of a talking cat he was actually kind of fun. "What's the first thing you'll do when you're human again, Vincent?"

Vincent sighed. "Drive a car. I've never driven one. I was enspelled before they were invented."

"Don't Nicholas and Darien take you for drives?"

"It's not the same thing. Besides, the last time I went driving with them I almost fell out of the car."

Nicholas almost choked on a chuckle. She turned to him, raising an eyebrow. "Almost fell out of the car?"

He shrugged, a delightfully mischievous grin pulling at his lips. "The top was down, the curve was sharp. I can't help it if he can't hold on." Nicholas swept past Vincent, opening the door that lead to the main level of the castle. "Maybe if you had curbed your tongue you would have been paying more attention and been better prepared."

Rebecca followed, moving close so she could whisper. "You deliberately tried to throw him from the car?"

"He may be a cat but he still has his magical powers. He could've gotten home with little difficulty."

"That's cold, Nicholas," she chastised.

"What happened to Nikki?" he teased. "And besides, spend a little time with him, you'll change your tune."

"Nikki?" she asked.

He smiled, sending chills of desire across her flesh. "You called me Nikki when you were smashed." He shrugged. "I liked it."

"Well if I call you Nikki what do I call Darien?"

Nicholas pursed his lips for a second. "A cab back to the mortal world?"

"If anyone is going back to the mortal world, *Nikki*," Darien snarled from the bottom of the main staircase. "It's you in the belly of a gornin."

"All right you two," Rebecca said with a sigh, admiring Darien in his jeans and turtleneck. God he looked good. The way the material of his shirt stretched across his chest, outlining all those glorious muscles, made her heart flutter. "What's a gornin?"

Vincent slinked past them, jumping up several stairs before coming to a stop. "A gornin is a small beast that resides in the protected dimension—similar to an oversized troll. They're carnivores, so they're kept from the mortal world."

Rebecca shuddered. "That is probably something I could have gone my whole life and not known existed."

Darien's deep chuckle washed over her flesh like a soft wave of cashmere. "Come on. Tonya and Marcus are waiting for us upstairs. If we leave them alone for too long we're liable to walk in on them having sex. They were all over each other a few moments ago like I wasn't even in the room."

With a smile Rebecca slipped her arm around Darien's elbow. Marcus was crazy about Tonya. She could see his love for her every time he looked at her friend. And Rebecca could certainly understand her total loss of control when it came to Marcus. She had the same feeling of helplessness when it came to her own men. They could do anything they wanted to her and she would go along more than willingly.

Slowly pushing open the heavy oak salon door, Rebecca scanned the room for her friend. A fire burned in the fireplace, casting soft flickering shadows around the room. Next to it stood Marcus and Tonya—her arms around his waist, her eyes sparkling with happiness as she smiled up at him. Marcus cupped her cheeks and leaned forward to gently kiss the tip of her nose. Rebecca's heart warmed for the two of them. Whether Tonya could see it yet or not they were perfect for each other.

Rebecca cleared her throat, getting their attention. "Are we shopping for dresses or having an orgy?" she asked with a cheeky grin.

"I vote for orgy," Darien replied with a grin and Rebecca slapped her hand across his hard stomach.

"Behave yourself."

Darien gasped playfully. "But where's the fun in that?"

"Exactly," Marcus drawled. Bending Tonya backward over his arm, he nibbled at the side of her neck with a growl. "I vote orgy too."

With a laugh, Tonya shoved at his shoulder, forcing him back up. "Dresses now." She wrapped her arms around his neck. "Making love later."

"Promise?" Marcus drawled, his lips spreading into a smile against Tonya's.

Rebecca smiled. "So, gentleman. What exactly are we looking for?"

Nicholas waved his hand, making an image appear in front of them. "Something black and elegant."

Rebecca studied the images. Men and women in their best formal outfits, a beautiful ballroom full of flickering candles and elegant white roses. The decorating was like something out of another era but the clothes were much more modern—black tuxedos for men and long black evening gowns for women. Diamonds of all shapes and sizes adorned their necks and wrists, glistening in the glow of the candles.

A man in one picture caught her attention. Long black hair surrounded an almost angelic face—perfectly sculpted with eyes the color of a clear summer sky that stared back at her, surrounded by long black lashes. He looked young, maybe early thirties. But also familiar.

"Who's that man?" Rebecca asked.

Marcus' lips thinned slightly. "That's my father, Jullian."

Rebecca studied Marcus, imagining him with longer hair. "I see the resemblance."

"Physically. That's about it."

Marcus moved to a small table in the corner and poured himself a drink from one of the crystal decanters. Tonya met her stare, concern etched on her face at Marcus' sudden withdrawal at the mention of his father. With a shrug, she indicated they should probably change the subject. Apparently Marcus didn't like talking about his father.

Turning back to the image, she noticed the sadness clouding Jullian's eyes and wondered what had caused it. Did Marcus know?

"Do you have an idea of what you want now?" Darien asked.

Rebecca shook her head with a sigh. "Maybe. What about you, Tonya?"

"I was thinking something off the shoulder."

"With a diamond choker," Marcus offered.

Tonya grinned. "You won't get any argument from me about diamonds."

Marcus strolled slowly around Tonya, eyeing her figure thoughtfully. "Let's see. You're about a size six, correct?"

Tonya's devilish gaze met Rebecca's. "Correct."

"How about this?"

Marcus waved his hand from Tonya's shoulder down to her calves. A black dress appeared on her tan body, off the shoulder, with a fitted waist and long narrow skirt, a diamond choker glistening around her neck. Tonya gasped. Placing her hands flat against her stomach, she stared down at the dress in awe.

"Oh. My. God. It's gorgeous."

"And it looks gorgeous on you," Rebecca said. She rushed to her friend's side and lifted her hair off her neck. "If you wear your hair up it will show off your neck and that amazing necklace."

Tonya lifted her hand to her throat. Turning, she admired herself in the mirror above the fireplace. "Are these real?"

"Of course," Nicholas replied.

Tonya's gaze met hers in the mirror. "You know what I think would look good on your figure?"

"What?"

With a grin, Tonya strolled over and whispered softly into Nicholas' and Darien's ears. Both men nodded, their eyes sparkling. Tilting her head, Rebecca studied them, smiling coyly and waiting for what her friend had in mind. Nicholas strolled over, letting his gaze wander down her body. Tingles worked their way along her spine, heating her flesh.

God, he looked so sexy when his eyes crinkled at the corners like that.

He brushed his hair back from his face with a swipe of his hand. "I think that will work," he murmured.

"What?" she asked, curious.

Nicholas winked and she started as the cool air of the room hit her bare arms. Glancing down, she noticed her clothes had changed. She no longer wore the jeans and t-shirt. Now she wore a beautiful long gown, its skirt full and flowing around her legs like a cloud. The waist was fitted, her back bare and the straps circled her neck, making a vee to dip low between her breasts. Sewn into the fabric of the skirt were diamonds that sparkled as she moved and swayed.

Around each wrist was a wide diamond bracelet and she lifted her hands, twirling her arms beneath the lights. "This is amazing," she said with a giggle. "How did you do that?"

"With a wink," Nicholas said, his lips twitching.

Darien stepped forward and grasped her hand, holding it up to kiss the backs of her fingers. Heat traveled up her arm as his full lips brushed across her skin. Desire flared in his gaze and her heart fluttered as she imagined all the things the three of them could do later.

"So where is the ball? In the protected dimension or in the mortal world?" she asked, forcing air past the sudden dryness in her throat.

"Mortal world," Nicholas replied as he brushed her hair over her shoulder. His fingers skimmed gently down her back, giving her goose bumps. "These dresses should go in your closet until then."

"What about the jewels?"

Darien leaned forward, his breath blowing enticingly against her ear as he spoke. "I think you should leave those on."

"Naked except for diamonds?" she mused. "Sounds intriguing."

Tonya giggled. As she strolled past with Marcus she placed her hand gently against Rebecca's arm. "Have fun."

Rebecca turned and stared at her friend with surprise. Oh my god. She'd completely forgotten Tonya was in the room. It amazed her what these two warlocks could do to her common sense.

"Are you leaving?" Rebecca asked.

"Just going to my room." She winked and slid her hand around Marcus' elbow. "I'll see you for breakfast? Usual place?"

With a nod, Rebecca smiled. "Usual time."

Wiggling her fingers, Tonya left with Marcus. Vincent, unusually quiet, jumped onto the sofa table and meowed. Darien sighed and turned to glare at the black cat watching them from his perch just behind the sofa. Vincent blinked, his stare unconcerned and downright haughty. Rebecca bit down on her lower lip to keep from smiling.

"Why don't you go raid the fishpond?" Darien snarled.

"Don't bother yelling if you fall in either," Nicholas added.

Rebecca pinched his side, narrowing her gaze at him.

"At least she takes up for me," Vincent pouted and Rebecca could have sworn she could see his lower lip stick out.

Darien snorted and scooped Vincent off the table. "She doesn't know you well enough yet."

"The two of you continually forget I'm more powerful than you are. Perhaps I should remind you of that fact."

"Knock yourself out." Darien snickered.

He tossed Vincent out the door. The cat recovered quickly. Landing on his feet, he turned to hiss back at them.

"That the best you got?" Darien queried.

With a flick of his hand the door shut with a bang, leaving Vincent on the other side.

Rebecca put her hands on her hips and turned to glare at the twins. "Why do the two of you dislike him so much?"

Nicholas shrugged. "We don't dislike him, not really. It's just that cat has been a pain in our asses since we were children. He needs to be put in his place every so often."

"Is he really more powerful than you?"

Darien pursed his lips as he trailed the backs of his fingers down her arm. "Probably."

Rebecca couldn't take her eyes off his as he watched her through his lashes. Sultry heat flared within their blue depths, making her pulse quicken.

"Aren't you afraid of him?" she asked.

"No." Darien shook his head. "He knows who feeds him."

"You're terrible," she giggled.

Nicholas moved to stand behind her and gently placed his hands against her shoulders. His fingers deftly unhooked the dress, allowing the material to fall and expose her breasts. Between the cool air of the room and Darien's heated stare her nipples hardened into tiny pebbles.

"In his present state his powers are weakened somewhat but if he were human he could definitely out cast all of us," Nicholas murmured then brushed his lips across the back of her shoulder.

Rebecca swallowed. "When is he supposed to become human again?"

"That's up to the council," Darien replied.

He tipped up her chin with his finger and swiped his tongue across her lower lip, making her shudder. Inhaling, she caught the whiff of warm brandy, cinnamon and hot, musky male. Darien pulled away and she leaned forward slightly to recapture his lips with hers. He chuckled and she opened her eyes to see him smiling at her devilishly. Prickles of desire moved along her skin as she imagined all the wild things his gaze promised.

He wagged his finger and her arms lifted over her head. She gasped, trying to move them, but something invisible held them immobile.

"If this bothers you let us know," Nicholas whispered in her ear.

Her heart beat rapidly in her chest as she rolled the whole idea through her mind. Did it bother her? No. In fact it turned her on even more. She'd never thought about being tied up by a lover but then again she'd also never thought her lovers would be powerful warlocks.

Glancing down, she saw her nipples pucker and a light pink flush move over her chest and breasts. They seemed to swell before her eyes, jutting outward, silently begging for the touch of her twin's hands.

"I, uh…I think I'm okay with it," she whispered.

Nicholas stroked his hand down her hip, pushing the delicate material of the dress down as he went, exposing her legs. Cool air washed between her thighs, stroking her aching pussy, making her hunger for so much more. Bending, Darien helped her to step out of the dress and gently laid it across the wingback chair closest to the fireplace.

Rebecca remained glued to the spot, her hands held captive above her. She could only stare helplessly as both men circled her naked body, fire blazing in their gazes. What did they have in mind? Her limbs trembled with growing need as she imagined the possibilities. Would they spank her? Would they tease her until she begged? She drew in a shaky breath. God, she hoped so.

Darien stopped before her. His long hair fell forward over his shoulder, the white streak mingling with the ebony black. His hair brushed across her nipple, making her shudder.

He eyed her through his lashes. "Does that feel good?"

She swallowed, nodding her head quickly. "Yes."

"What about this?" His tongue flicked across her nipple and she gasped as white-hot heat settled deep in her stomach.

Passion and desire like this was something she'd never imagined she would find. She'd dreamed of it—read about it in books but never thought she'd ever feel it herself. The intensity was more than she could handle at times—the need to feel them both inside her almost strangling the very life from her. Could something that felt this good be real?

Nicholas dropped to his knees behind her and gently nipped at the rise of her hips, his palms slowly spreading her thighs. Two fingers slid enticingly along her slit to glide through the juices coating her pussy.

"Is this for real?" she murmured, her eyes closing on a sigh.

Darien rose to brush his lips across hers. "It's a real as it gets. This isn't magic, sweet. This is us."

His palms moved around to cup her breasts. His fingers pinched at her nipples, the sharp pain sending tingles down her spine. Darien cupped her pussy with one hand smiling as her cream leaked onto his fingers.

"Such a wet pussy," he purred. "Do you like being bound?"

"Yes," she sighed.

"Would you like for me to eat your pussy while you're bound?"

Rebecca's whole body burst into flames at the mere mention of his mouth on her dripping mound. His fingers moved away and her hips thrust forward in search of his touch again.

"Answer me," he murmured. His tongue licked across her lips, making her whimper. "Answer me and I'll replace my hand with my mouth."

"Yes. Lick me, Darien."

Her fingers trembled, clutching and unclutching at the invisible force holding them up. She waited, panting and tense, for Darien to lick her, to feel his hot mouth against her mound. He knelt and spread her thighs wide. She sucked in a shocked gulp of air as her feet left the floor but relaxed as she realized another invisible force held her, allowing her lower body to float.

Her legs lifted to his shoulders as he leaned forward and swiped his tongue along her slit. She hissed, her hips bucking wildly. His hot breath blew against her, teasing her, tormenting her. Nicholas moved around, his gaze lazily watching as his fingers worked the buttons of his shirt free.

Rebecca's heart felt as though it would burst from her chest it pounded so hard. Darien continued the slow, leisurely swipes of his tongue through the juices of her pussy, making her mindless with need. With quickening desire she watched Nicholas drop his pants, freeing his engorged shaft. The purple head dripped with pre-cum and she licked her lips, remembering his salty taste.

His gaze met hers and the heat emanating from his eyes almost singed her flesh.

"I like watching you," he purred as he moved forward and placed his hand on Darien's shoulder. "I like watching your face as Darien licks your pussy."

"Oh god," Rebecca sighed as her body shuddered from head to toe.

Darien's fingers spread her labia. His tongue lapped at her cream, the tip gently circling her clit to toy with her. She screamed, both in pleasure and frustration. The torment felt so good.

"My turn," Nicholas growled and Darien stood, allowing his brother to drop between her splayed thighs and lick his fill as well. But before he walked away Darien thrust two fingers deep into her pussy, making her gasp and thrust her hips upward.

Nicholas groaned and licked around her clit, adding his two fingers as well. She gulped in air, her body shivering with delight. She wanted them to end this torture but at the same time didn't want them to stop. Darien removed his fingers and moved behind her, where his hands gently massaged her ass. Slowly his fingers worked their way to the tight puckered hole of her anus then gently slid inside past the ring of resistance.

Rebecca almost shattered. "Please," she gasped. "Oh god."

"You taste so good, baby," Nicholas purred as he continued to lick at her juices and fuck her with his fingers.

Every part of her burned with the need to orgasm. She could feel it just out of reach. Her body tensed and trembled, her pussy creamed and spasmed. But both of them held her back, kept her from reaching that pinnacle, and she thought she would die if they didn't stop—if they didn't let her come.

"That's it, sweet. Cream for him. Cream for me," Darien purred in her ear, his teeth nipping gently on her lobe, his fingers tormenting her ass.

"Nicholas, please. Please fuck me."

Nicholas stood, adjusting her legs around his waist. Her hands were still bound above, her body still floating as though weightless. "I'll give you what you want but you can't come."

"What?" she gasped, unsure she could stop herself.

"I mean it. No coming. Understand?"

She nodded, her gaze glued to his intense one. How in god's name would she pull that off? How would she keep herself from shattering? Darien removed his fingers from her ass and held her back steady as Nicholas rammed into her with the full length of his cock. Her body tensed as she tried to hold back—tried to do as he'd asked of her. Every inch of him stretched and filled her pussy as he pulled out only to thrust forward even deeper.

She cried out, lifting her hips against his, totally engulfed in the pleasure racing through her.

He pulled back and she whimpered at the loss. "Don't come," Nicholas growled.

"I don't think I can stop it," she murmured.

"You can," Darien whispered in her ear and with a nod he and Nicholas traded places again.

Darien lifted her legs then, slowly, keeping his eyes locked on hers the whole time, slid his cock deep inside her. His eyes closed briefly as he seated himself balls deep, his thick girth stretching her wide and filling her so full she thought she might bust.

"God, you feel good," he groaned then began to move, his slow thrusts torturing her beyond her wildest imagination.

She wanted it harder. She wanted to feel him lose himself in it. She wanted to feel both of them buried inside her. Nicholas waved his hand, releasing her wrists. She let them fall to Darien's shoulders, feeling the muscles flex and bunch beneath her touch. She didn't need to hold on, still remained levitating, but she needed to touch him, wanted to feel the heat of his flesh.

Nicholas pressed against her back, pushing her closer to Darien. She knew what he was about to do and she wanted it. Oh yes, she wanted it. Darien stilled, allowing Nicholas time to press his thick cock into her ass.

He stroked the palm of his hand over his cock, using magic to spread a thin sheen of lubricant, then pressed forward. Rebecca tensed slightly at the harsh burning as he stretched the tight ring, filling her full. The pain soon passed, leaving her with an incredible sensation of pleasure that almost sent her over the edge.

"Oh yes," she hissed, sagging back against Nicholas.

They both began to move, gently at first then harder, faster, their thrusts timed in perfect unison. Rebecca could do nothing but ride out the wave, allowing their emotions and feelings to flow through her, fill her, consume her. Nicholas grunted, his breath coming hard and fast in her ear.

"Come for us now, baby. Let us feel it."

It didn't take much and as soon as he allowed her she let her release go. With a scream loud enough to wake the dead she rode out the sensations. The pounding thrusts of their cocks sent her higher, soaring over anything she'd ever felt before. Every part of her screamed in pleasure and pain, every nerve ending prickled with release. Her legs shook from the intensity while her pussy and ass clenched tightly along the invading shafts.

"Oh, fuck yeah," Darien shouted, then with a final thrust emptied his seed deep inside her. Nicholas followed seconds later, his cock spasming inside her as he lost himself to his own release.

Rebecca couldn't move. Didn't know if she even wanted to. All she knew was that she didn't want this to ever end.

Chapter Ten

❧

Heat. Intense heat surrounded her, made sweat trickle down her back. The smell of burning flesh filled her nose and she swallowed to keep from vomiting. Squinting, she tried to see into the darkness engulfing her. There was nothing. Only smells and sounds – horrible sounds – filling the air around her and she shivered in fear.

Horrible, pain-laced screams filled her ears and she jerked around, searching through the pitch-black for the cause. Ahead of her dim red light cut its way through a foggy haze of smoke. With growing trepidation she slowly walked toward it, her eyes ever watchful.

Her fingers shook as they reached out, touching the rock wall next to her, the cold of the stone a stark contrast to the heat flowing through the cavern.

She was in the bowels of hell. She had to be.

A form began to take shape ahead of her. Tall and slim, he slowly became more in focus the closer she went. Fear tightened her chest and she froze, unable to move any closer. Her heart pounded in her chest as the shadowy form moved closer. She took a step back, retreating from the danger she sensed.

"You can't get away from me, Rebecca," he snarled, his voice rough and gravely, full of command and hatred.

"What do you want from me?" she demanded.

The figure moved forward with a flash of inhuman speed. She gasped as his face filled her vision, the evil in his light blue eyes taunting her. "Your death," he sneered.

She closed her eyes, screaming loudly.

Nicholas awoke with a jolt, turning quickly to find Rebecca sitting up in the bed, her fingers clutching the sheet, her voice screaming her distress. Darien sat up as well, his hands reaching out to grasp her shoulders.

"Rebecca," Nicholas yelled as he too turned and cupped her face. "Hey, baby. Wake up."

She stopped screaming and stared at him. Her eyes wide with fear, her brow covered in sweat.

"What happened?" he whispered.

Darien leaned forward and wrapped his arms around her shoulders as Rebecca began to shiver from head to toe.

"He wanted to kill me," she whispered. "He'd brought me to hell to kill me."

Brushing her hair from her forehead, he shared a troubled glance with Darien. Her mother had been able to glimpse small flashes of the future. Was it possible Rebecca has that same ability? Or was it just a nightmare brought on by stress?

"You're okay, baby," Darien whispered. "It was just a nightmare."

Shaking her head, Rebecca wiped at the tears escaping her eyes with shaking fingers. "No. It wasn't. I've seen him before."

"Seen who before?" Nicholas asked.

"The man in my dream. I saw him before I met you. The night before I went to the club. What does Sebastian look like?"

"Shoulder length gray hair and light blue eyes."

"Tall and slim?" she asked, her eyes widening. Darien's did as well, though Rebecca couldn't see him.

Nicholas brushed his thumb across her cheek. "It's a coincidence."

"No," she murmured, shaking her head.

Cupping her cheeks, Nicholas forced her to look at him. "Listen to me, Becca. He won't hurt you. I swear it."

She licked her lips, nodding. But he could tell by the terrified look in her eyes she didn't believe him. He pulled her into his arms, holding her trembling body close to him. Falling back, he pulled her with him while Darien covered them with the blanket then he curled at her back, his arm snaking around her waist to hold her from the other side.

It took a long time for her shaking to subside. Finally she fell into a fitful sleep but Nicholas and his brother remained awake—watchful.

Nicholas' gut tightened in fear. He'd never loved a woman. Never allowed himself to get close enough to one. He'd known his fate. He'd known his wife had already been ordained by fate, picked out for him. He'd just never imagined he'd find himself so crazy about her. And so damn close to losing her. His arms tightened around her, hardening his resolve to keep her alive.

"If anything happens to her, Nicholas..." Darien whispered.

He didn't finish the sentence. He didn't have to. Nicholas knew well how desperate Darien was to keep her safe. It was the same desperation that kept him awake at night. The same desperation that kept him strengthening spells and delving into forbidden territory—black magic.

* * * * *

"What's wrong?"

Rebecca looked up from her cup of coffee to find Tonya standing across the table, staring down at her in concern. Her friend pulled out the chair and sat down, waiting patiently for her to spill her guts. A small grin tugged at Rebecca's lips. She was so glad her friend was here.

Rebecca's finger traced the edge of her delicate bone china coffee cup. It shook slightly and she clenched her hands, trying to make it stop. She'd been doing that all morning. Shaking, peeking around every corner, checking empty closets. She expected the man from her dream to jump out any minute and drag her off to some hell she couldn't even begin to imagine.

"I had a terrible nightmare last night." She swallowed, her gaze glued to the steam floating off the coffee. "But I think it was more than that." She lifted her eyes, staring with fear at Tonya. "I think I saw my future."

"What did you see?"

"A cave. Fire, smoke. And the screams." Resting her elbows on the table, she leaned forward and covered her mouth. Bile rumbled through her stomach as the images again ran through her mind. "They were so terrible. So..."

Tonya reached across the table and touched her arm gently. "Sweetie, it was just a nightmare."

"No." Rebecca shook her head stubbornly. "It was more than that. It was real. I could feel the heat, Tonya. Really feel it. And the man in my dream. I think he was Sebastian."

"Why don't we go for a walk?" Tonya suggested. "It's a gorgeous morning. Maybe it will take your mind off of it."

Nodding reluctantly, Rebecca stood and followed Tonya to the garden path. Maybe Tonya was right. Maybe it was just a nightmare and she was letting her imagination run away with her.

No. She just couldn't accept that.

"How was your night with Marcus?" Rebecca asked, trying to take her mind off the dream and the nagging fear deep in her gut.

She had a terrible feeling something was about to happen but didn't have a clue what. Gazing around, she took in the blooming flowers and bright blue sky. God it was beautiful here.

"As good as always," Tonya replied with a grin. "I'm beginning to get used to the whole vampire thing."

Rebecca turned to study her friend, trying to see if she really meant what she'd just said. "Are you sure?"

Tonya's shoulder lifted slightly in a shrug. "I think so. I can't imagine going home without him now. Am I crazy?" she asked, meeting her gaze. "Would I be nuts to even consider it?"

"Not if you love him."

"But would the love last an eternity? Would we still love each other two hundred years from now?"

Rebecca snorted, her lips lifting in the first real grin since she'd gotten out of bed. "I believe the two of you would."

Tonya sighed and glanced toward the sky. "It's all happened so fast, hasn't it?

"I know. It's almost scary."

Tonya raised her hand, shielding her eyes from the sunlight as she stared intently at something in the sky. "Speaking of scary. What the hell is that?"

Rebecca looked as well. Two large birds headed toward them, their wings spread wide. Their large grayish bodies resembled bats. Dread seeped into her bones and her stomach knotted with apprehension. Something wasn't right, she could feel it—smell it.

Reaching out, she touched Tonya's arm. "Go," she murmured, then shouted louder, "Go! Now! Run!"

They both turned and took off down the path back toward the castle. Her heart pounded wildly in her chest as the realization that they were here for her sank in. She knew it. She had to get back to the castle but it was too far away.

Grabbing Tonya's elbow, she stopped her friend and pulled her close. She'd never tried transporting before...wasn't even sure she could do it but she had to give it a try. The bats were bearing down on them, their wings silent as they glided through the air, coming closer every second. She closed her eyes, trying to concentrate, trying to picture the lab.

Suddenly a force shoved at her chest. She and Tonya flew apart, landing in the grass about twenty yards from each other. Pain laced through her limbs, sharp tingles of pain either from the force of the fall to the ground or whatever it was that had shoved at her chest. She gulped for air, trying to sit up and make sure Tonya was okay.

Her friend struggled to her knees, her face pale. "No, stay down," Rebecca called out. Maybe if Tonya remained motionless whatever those things were would leave her alone.

A shadow passed over her body and she glanced up warily at the demonic creatures now towering over her, tall and massive. Their eyes glowed red and she cringed at the horrid smell surrounding her. She gasped with shock. She remembered that smell. It was the same burning flesh smell from her dream.

Panting now, she began to back away across the lawn, scooting on her ass and palms. Behind them she saw Tonya raise a branch, preparing to swing it at one of the creatures. Without even turning around the creature waved his hand, forcing Tonya to the ground. She landed hard on her back. With a groan she rolled to her side.

Panic set in, chilling Rebecca to her core. She had to do something. Concentrating, she tried to freeze them using the spell Nicholas had taught her. "*Vilat,*" she cried.

It didn't work. With a growl, one of the bats raised its palm, forcing her to float off the ground and toward them. She struggled against it, against its power and the invisible force pulling her along but she wasn't strong enough. Her powers were too weak, too unused.

One of them wrapped its claws around her neck, holding her close to its face. She cringed, trying not to inhale for fear of gagging from their stench. Heat poured off them in waves. Intense, burning heat. She tried to pull away from it but they held her closer, wrapping their wings around her.

"No," she cried.

Shaking her head, she kicked out her feet, trying to hit anything that might help her to get away but it was no use. A flash of light preceded a sharp pain throughout her body. She cried out, disappearing along with the demons.

* * * * *

Tonya tried to stand, shaking off the pounding at the back of her head. The clearing where Rebecca and those creatures had been was now empty. Fear made her shake but at the same time gave her strength. Pushing off the ground, Tonya fought against the tears and stumbled toward the house, screaming for Marcus as loudly as she could.

Just as she reached the steps to the veranda all three men, including the cat, came barreling out the door.

"My god," Marcus growled as he rushed forward to help her. "What happened?"

"They took Rebecca," she cried, tears streaming down her face.

"Who took Rebecca?" Nicholas asked, his voice shaking with fear.

She glanced up at him, guilt eating away at her stomach. "I'm so sorry. I tried to stop them."

"Who?" Darien demanded, his face pale.

She shook her head, wishing she could tell them more than she could. "I don't know. They looked like bats."

Nicholas went ashen. Darien stood and grabbed a coffee cup of the table. With an angry growl, he threw it against the stone wall of the castle. It shattered, falling to the floor in hundreds of tiny pieces. Anger raged through his whole body, tensing it, making his eyes glow dangerously.

"Demons," Vincent murmured.

Tonya shuddered and Marcus wrapped his arm around her. "Demons? But how did they get in here?"

"They're the only ones that can," Marcus replied with a sigh. "Not even black magic can keep them out."

Anger rolled through her as she stared at Nicholas. He leaned against the wall, bending over with his hands against his knees. He was devastated. Angry. Terrified. She could see it in every inch of his body, in the anguish shining in his eyes as he stood straight against the wall, his gaze fastened on the sky above them.

"Why didn't you think of this?" she demanded, focusing her anger on Nicholas. Even though deep down she knew it wasn't his fault. "Why didn't you do something to protect her?"

Nicholas closed his eyes, his lips thinning into a tight line. Darien continued to pace, anger tensing his body.

Vincent stepped forward and waved his front paw at her. "We had no idea Sebastian was in league with demons. He's apparently much more powerful than any of us imagined."

"So now what?" she demanded.

Marcus tried to console her but she pushed his hand away in agitation. She wouldn't be treated like a damn child. She wanted something done and she wanted it done now.

"What are you going to do to get her back?"

"If demons were involved she was taken to hell. If that's the case I don't know if we can get her back." Vincent replied sadly and Tonya gaped at him in shock. "We cannot gain access to the caverns without a demon leading the way,"

She shook her head, refusing to accept his answer as that. "There has to be a way. What about your black magic? Isn't there a spell you could cast?"

Nicholas stood straighter, his eyes widening slightly. Pushing away from the wall, he headed inside.

"No, Nicholas," Vincent snarled.

"What?" Tonya demanded as they all followed a silent Nicholas to his lab in the basement.

Nicholas stormed into the lab, anger and regret eating him alive. Why had he let her go the gardens alone? He'd had a bad feeling all morning after that nightmare she had. He should have listened more to his instincts. The others followed quickly behind, each filing into the room silently

With an angry wave of his hand he brought up a spell, the words hanging in the air before him.

"It will take three of us," Nicholas murmured, studying the spell.

Vincent jumped onto the counter, his tail swishing angrily. "You cannot do this, Nicholas. It's one thing to dabble in black magic, it's just frowned upon, but you cannot use a forbidden spell. It would mean banishment for you. For all of us."

"I don't give a fuck."

"Think about what you're doing," Vincent cautioned.

The anger within him finally burst and he turned to yell at Vincent. "I will not lose her! If it means my banishment then so be it!"

"What if it means your execution?" Vincent yelled back.

Nicholas stared down at him, his jaw tightening and flexing in anger. It didn't matter anymore. All that mattered was getting her out of there. She wasn't strong enough to battle Sebastian alone. She wouldn't survive.

"I can't just sit here and do nothing, Vincent. I can't. She means everything to me and I have to get her back."

Vincent remained silent then nodded in resigned understanding.

"What do we need?" Darien asked as he stepped forward and began rummaging through the various herbs and jars.

Nicholas turned slightly and waved his hand, forming another list of words next to the original spell. "The list is here."

"You said it would take three," Marcus replied softly from his spot by the door.

Vincent raised his palm. "I'll do it. I'm more powerful than you, Marcus. Besides, I'm already in trouble. What's a little casting of a forbidden spell?"

Marcus shook his head as though to argue but Nicholas held up his hand, stopping him. A sad smile tugged at his lips. "You're Jullian's son, Marcus. We may be able talk our way out of this with the council. You wouldn't stand a chance and you know it."

His gaze turned to Tonya, who stood next to Marcus, tears streaming down her face. His gut clenched at the worry he saw in her eyes, guilt ate away at him, leaving almost nothing in its wake but determination. Rebecca was his life. He would die without her. He knew that now and also knew his brother felt the same way. He could see it in his tortured gaze.

"We'll get her back, I promise."

* * * * *

Rebecca's stomach roiled with nausea as she tried to sit up. Rocks bit into her back and hips, heat singed her skin. She coughed, gagging on the acrid smell filling the thick air. Where was she?

Opening her eyes, she stared in fear at the place she'd seen in her dream—the cavern, the screams, the heat. Demons hovered close by, their glowing eyes watching her with morbid fascination. Blood dripped from the rocks surrounding her, adding to the acrid smell. Fear snaked through her, making her tremble. She had to find a way out. She had to get back to Nicholas and Darien.

She couldn't leave them, not now. She loved them. Loved them with everything she had in her. She wanted to live, not die here in this place—not at Sebastian's hands.

Moving to her knees, she winced as the hard ground bit into her flesh. She tried to better make out her surroundings but steam and smoke surrounded her. In the distance the steam glowed red. The screams echoed around her. She covered her ears, trying to block them out but it was no use. They came from everywhere, even from inside her mind.

Sobbing, she dropped her hands to the ground, feeling for anything she could use to make a capture circle, praying it would work here. Her hands only met hard, solid ground. No pebbles, no dirt. Nothing. In anger, she slapped her hand against the ground, her sobs coming harder now.

She hated herself for crying. Hated that weakness but she couldn't stop. All she could think about were Nicholas and Darien. Her twin warlocks. Her loves.

"I expected more."

Glancing up, she met Sebastian's ice-cold eyes. He stood a few feet away, a cape around his shoulders, long grayish-blond hair falling over one shoulder, a cane in his hand. At the top of it the glowing red eyes of a dragon stared toward her, flickering as though they were alive. She shuddered at the evil that surrounded her, choked her.

"Fuck you," she snarled.

"Not today, I'm afraid," he purred, sending tingles of fear down her spine.

"What do you want from me?"

He squatted, bringing himself eye level. She couldn't stop the gnawing hatred that gripped her. The anger. This man killed her parents—wanted to kill her.

"Your death," he hissed and she gasped. She'd seen this. She was reliving her nightmare.

Reaching out, he grabbed her wrist roughly, turning it so the underside faced the ceiling. "Such beautiful skin," he murmured as his fingers gently caressed the inside of her wrist.

She flinched, trying to pull her hand from his gasp. He held tight, the force of his hold tightening and hurting her fingers.

"It will be a shame to see it slashed."

She gasped, narrowing her eyes at him. "They'll know you did it. Nicholas and Darien will see to it that they know."

Sebastian snorted. "All they'll see when they meld with you is your own suicide."

A chill ran down Rebecca's spine. Glancing down, she spotted a long jagged knife in her left hand. She stared in shock, unsure where it had come from but immediately knowing what she was to do with it. She shook her head, glaring at Sebastian.

"No," she growled as her hand moved closer to the wrist Sebastian held. He was making her do it, making her kill herself.

She struggled against his power. His mind was so much stronger than hers, his powers so much more refined. She couldn't fight him and cried out as the blade bit into her flesh, sinking deep within her wrist. Burning pain raced up her arm as her warm blood spilled onto the ground with every beat of her pulse.

"No," she gasped.

Wrenching her wrist from his hand she dropped the knife and tried to cover the gaping wound.

Sebastian laughed at her futile efforts. "There's no stopping it now, child. You'll die, having killed yourself over your failure to accept what you are."

"They'll never believe it," she hissed, her voice sounding far away even to her own ears.

Fatigue pulled at her shoulders and coldness seeped into her flesh, making her shiver. She couldn't stop the flow of blood as it spurted to the ground. As she watched, ignoring Sebastian's laughter, she remembered the circle. It could be made from anything. Even her own blood?

Glancing back at Sebastian, she moved carefully, slowly. She only had about a minute at best. She had to do this without him catching on.

"*Borlasie*," she murmured under her breath as she held her wrist out, letting the blood drip to the ground. "*Borlasie*," she repeated, turning slowly so that the blood dripped around her in what she hoped was a circle.

Sebastian smiled, unaware of what she was doing. His gaze had moved to the ceiling, his mouth spreading into a triumphant grin. "Your seat will be mine, the vampires will control the council and you, my dear, will be the last of your line."

She glanced up at him in anger, her mind fading, her limbs growing numb. "Not if I can help it."

With on final swipe of her wrist, she closed the circle. "*Borlasie*," she whispered and a blue haze appeared around her, enclosing her.

Sebastian's eyes widened and he took a step toward her. "No," he growled. "You're not strong enough."

She closed her eyes, concentrating with all her might on home. On her twins. "Nicholas!" she screamed then fainted as a blinding light consumed her.

* * * * *

Darien shoved bottles aside in aggravation. Where was that damn bottle of jasmine? He was so worried about Rebecca he could hardly think. They had to find her. They had to get her back. He needed her. He hadn't even realized how much until just now. He vowed if they got her back, he'd tell. He'd tell her how he felt. How much he loved her.

"Rebecca!" Tonya screamed and Darien dropped the jar he'd just picked up. It fell to the floor, shattering as he turned to see what had made Tonya scream.

He froze, unable to breathe as he stared at a pale, unconscious Rebecca on the floor. "Oh my god," he cried as he dropped to his knees next to her.

Fear unlike anything he'd ever known swam through him, tightening his chest. Blood slowly oozed from her wrist and he lifted her hand, quickly grabbing a towel to hold over the gaping wound and stop the bleeding. Nicholas dropped to the floor on her other side, his hands cupping her face.

"My god, she's so cold," he murmured. "Becca, come on, baby, talk to me."

"She's lost too much blood," Vincent said from the counter. "Marcus. Get the vermillion off the top shelf. Quickly. And get some of that salve to close her wrist."

Marcus jumped to do his bidding. Tonya moved to sit at Rebecca's knees, her lips trembling with unshed tears, her frightened gaze glued to Rebecca's wounded wrist. "Why would she do that?"

"She didn't," Nicholas hissed. "I'm going to kill that son of a bitch."

"How did she get out of there?" Vincent murmured.

"I taught her to do a capture circle," Nicholas replied.

"She was able to transport from Hell?" Darien gasped and glanced toward Vincent. "Can Rebecca really be that strong?"

Marcus dropped down next to Darien and handed him the salve, which would harden and hold the wound on her wrist closed.

"Her father was. It's possible she inherited his strength. It's also possible she just wanted it badly enough. Her desire gave her strength."

Darien and Nicholas both stared down at her while Marcus administered the vermillion into her system. That along with the other herbs he'd mixed in should save her, provided she'd gotten here in time. She looked so pale, so weak, Darien's heart broke. He would trade places with her in a flat second if it were possible.

Leaning down, he brushed her hair from her brow and placed a soft kiss on her forehead. It was cold to his touch. Like death. "Don't leave us, baby. Don't leave *me*."

* * * * *

"Aahhhhh!" Sebastian howled, his arms stretched out in anger.

How the hell did she do it? How the hell did she pull it off without him fucking seeing her? And how the hell did she get that strong?

"So you want to make it difficult, do you, you little bitch?" he shouted through the smoke, his rage changing into determination. "Fine. I look forward to killing you slowly."

Chapter Eleven

80

Darien paced the quiet bedroom, his nerves on edge, his heart breaking for the pale woman lying in his bed. Nicholas sat next to her, holding her hand, constantly rechecking her pulse to make sure it steadily climbed. Darien couldn't sit that still. He needed to hit something, break it, smash it until every ounce of murderous rage was out of his system.

Vincent lay at the foot of the bed, his eyes ever watchful, his control and level-headedness for once a godsend. Tonya stood at the dresser, leaning against it as she kept her worried gaze on her friend. Marcus remained close to her, offering support for her quiet sobs.

It had been two hours since she'd returned. Two hours of waiting and watching. Hoping.

"Darien," Nicholas whispered and he turned to see Rebecca stir amid the covers.

His heart stopped as he moved to sit on her other side. Taking her still-cold hand in his, he watched her eyelids flutter gently.

"Rebecca," he whispered.

She mumbled, tossing her head to the side with a frown.

Nicholas brushed her hair from her brow. "Becca, baby. You're safe."

Her eyes opened and she stared at them groggily. Tonya's whispered, "thank god," floated over to them and Darien smiled slightly.

"You're going to be okay, sweet. You did it."

"How did you do it?" Nicholas asked softly, his lips placing gentle kisses against the back of her hand.

"I thought of you two." Her eyes closed, her lashes fluttering gently against her pale cheeks. "I love you," she whispered.

Darien's heart soared and he dropped his head to the mattress next to her. She loved him. He could fly, he swore he could. "I love you, too, sweet," he whispered, placing a soft kiss against her brow.

Nicholas sat across from him, his head bent, Rebecca's hand held against his forehead. Sniffing and blinking back tears, Nicholas stood then bent to place a kiss on her cheek. "Sleep, sweet baby. We'll be right here."

"She's regained consciousness. That's a very good sign," Vincent reported as he rose to all fours. "Let's let her get some rest. Darien, you stay with her. Nicholas and I have some casting to do."

Nicholas nodded, reluctantly following Vincent from the room. Tonya and Marcus left as well, saying they would return later to check on her. Climbing onto the bed, Darien enfolded Rebecca into his arms, holding her close. He closed his eyes and listened to the soft, even breathing of her sleep, the gentle thumping of her heart.

"*Mira tiesla*," he murmured, raising an invisible shield of protection around him and Rebecca. That would keep her safe for the time being and alert him to any more demon intrusions. To hell with the council and their restrictions on black magic. She was his life. He refused to take any more chances.

* * * * *

Tonya slumped against the closed bedroom door, so relieved her friend would be okay she wanted to cry. Rebecca was all she had in this world—other than Marcus.

Her gaze moved to him as he pulled back the covers of the bed. He crossed his arms, grabbing his shirt at the hem and lifting it over his head. Her gaze wandered over his hard, smooth chest and the thick ridges of his stomach. He was so beautiful, his skin and body perfect, his eyes piercing and seductive.

As she watched him she remembered the picture she'd seen of his father the other night. Jullian had that same unreal beauty about him, those same piercing eyes.

"Are all vampires like you and your father?" she asked.

He looked up at her, his fingers frozen on the button fly of his jeans. "What do you mean?"

"Beautiful."

His lips quirked in amusement. "You think I'm beautiful?"

She rolled her eyes. "You are and you know it." Smiling gently, she continued, "You and your father both have this...unreal beauty about you."

"I can assure you I'm real." His voice dropped an octave, sending waves of desire up her spine. "Come here and I'll show you just how real."

Her lips twitched slightly but she kept her spot by the door. She wanted answers and she knew if she got any closer to him answers would be the last thing on her mind. He had that much control over her.

"I'm serious, Marcus. I want to know about you. About your kind." She met his gaze head-on. "I need to know."

He nodded. "All right." Leaving the fly of his jeans buttoned, he sat on the edge of the bed, facing her. Did he sense she needed this space?

"Ummm. Yes. All vampires have an ethereal beauty about them, although not all vampires are good. Some of the most beautiful are the most evil. Some, like my father, just exist the best they can, floating between the mortal world and the protected dimension the warlocks created thousands of years ago."

"So your father isn't one of the evil ones."

Marcus shrugged. "He has a formidable reputation. He's well over eight hundred years old and I think he's mellowed somewhat with age but in his younger time, I've heard, he was quite the force to be reckoned with. Some still fear him today. He still has this," Marcus waved his hand, trying to think of the right words, "this evil quality about him. But I like to believe that deep down he's a good man."

"What about your mother?"

"She died several hundred years ago." He watched her closely. "She couldn't bring herself to change over."

"Why?" Tonya whispered.

"She told me before she died that she regretted that decision. She loved him. Missed him but she was afraid. Afraid she wouldn't be able to do what she had to to feed."

Tonya nodded, understanding that fear.

"It would be different for us, Tonya. I don't feed. I don't need to. And neither will you."

"How do you know?"

"I've never turned anyone but I know a half-breed who has. She became what he was and I believe that's the way it will be with us."

"But you've fed from me."

"Only from you. You are the first woman I've ever slept with who I felt the need to bite." Marcus stood and slowly walked toward her. "I won't deny that I like the taste of blood. I like your taste but I don't *crave* it. Maybe it's because I'm only half, maybe it's something my mother did. I don't know."

He stopped in front of her, his eyes glowing with love and desire. For her. Her heart warmed and a lot of her resolve melted away but still some smart part of her fought it. Fought what she knew she wanted more than anything. And that was to spend eternity with him.

After today she knew without a doubt how much she loved him but she was still so damn afraid.

He gently cupped her cheeks, tilting her head up. "All I know, Tonya, is that I love you," he whispered against her lips, his breath warm and enticing it as it blew across her mouth. "I love you with everything that I am."

His mouth brushed across her, sending sparks straight to her core. Her lips parted but he didn't deepen the kiss. Instead he teased, using his tongue to trace the edges of her lips to explore her teeth and the inside of her lip. She whimpered at the sensual play—the way he coaxed her tongue into responding.

With a deep growl of satisfaction he dipped his tongue into her mouth, mating with hers. She melted at the tender onslaught, the gentle way his lips molded to hers, the taste of him as their mouths mated.

Lifting her hands, she braced them at his waist, her nails softly scraping across his flesh. His body was warm and she wanted more of that heat, needed it to fill her and make her whole. His lips moved to the sensitive spot behind her ear and his teeth scratched across her skin, making her gasp. Closing her eyes, she tilted her head further to the side, allowing him better access.

"Marcus," she sighed, but instead of biting her, he moved down along the column of her throat.

Shivers worked their way down her spine and her knees grew weak. Marcus moved closer, pressing her against the door. She moaned as his chest brushed across her nipples. Even through the material of her clothes the touch of his body against hers had the ability to send sparks to her womb.

Cream leaked from her pussy and she wiggled, lifting one leg to encircle his thigh. Marcus growled, the sound primal, as he dipped slightly and pressed his hard cock into the hungry vee of her thighs.

"Will it always be like this?" she wondered aloud.

Marcus pulled away slightly, his eyes glazed from passion, his lips full and so delectable. "Always, Tonya. I promise."

Bending, he put a hand behind her knees and swung her into his arms. She squealed, her lips spreading into a full smile as he carried her to the bed.

"Do you realize this will be the first time we've made love in a bed?" she whispered, her nose brushing across the skin under his ear. Parting her lips, she scraped her teeth across his flesh. Marcus stiffened, coming to a stop at the foot of the bed.

"What's it like to bite?"

"Tonya," he croaked, his breath now coming in short pants.

She eyed him through her lashes, trying to gauge this sudden change. His whole body felt tense, ready to pounce and his eyes flashed fire hot as the sun. "I love—"

"Remember what I told you," he interrupted, his gaze intent, scorching. "If you say it you better be sure."

"Because once I do I'm yours," she finished for him. Leaning forward, she licked her tongue across his bottom lip. "I want to be yours. All yours. Forever. I love you, Marcus."

With an animalistic growl he threw her onto the bed. Climbing to her knees, she watched in awe as he shoved his pants down, freeing his massive shaft. God he was magnificent. Fisting her shirt in his hand, he tugged her to him. His lips descended, catching her mouth in a kiss that left her utterly breathless.

Never breaking the kiss, he tugged at her shirt with both hands, ripping it in two. She gasped, breaking away to stare down at herself. Marcus pulled it from her shoulders and threw it to the floor.

Her pulse pounded through her veins. His gaze locked with hers. His blue eyes seemed to glow with an inner light but it didn't frighten her. Instead it intensified her lust. No one had ever looked at her like that—like they could eat her alive.

The realization that Marcus could very well eat her alive made her flesh tingle as though on fire.

"Fuck the clothes," he growled and with a wave of his hand she was naked.

"Wow," she said, her lips lifting in a slight grin. "You certainly don't waste any time, do you?"

"Shut up, woman," he snarled but she didn't miss the flicker of devilment in his gaze.

"Make me," she purred back.

He climbed onto the bed with her, balancing himself on his knees. "Oh I'll make you all right," he growled, his voice deep and seductive.

Raising his hand, he shoved at her chest, sending her sprawling backward onto the bed. Settling between her thighs, he pressed the tip of his cock into her aching pussy. Her hips lifted, begging for more but he held back for just a second.

"That and then some," he growled just before shoving his cock inside her balls-deep.

She screamed, lifting her hips to meet his powerful thrusts. He was so big, so powerful all she could do was hold on for dear life and take what he gave her. It felt so good, his cock stretching her, filling her as he pounded into her over and over.

His mouth covered hers, swallowing her groans. Her tongue flicked across his fangs as they descended, the sharp edges piercing her. The metallic taste of blood filled her mouth. Marcus groaned and sucked greedily. His hunger for her was the most erotic thing she'd ever felt. A desperate need to taste him began to build deep inside her. She wanted him to be a part of her, just like she was a part of him.

She couldn't think this through anymore. She wanted him. She wanted to be with him. Forever.

"Marcus," she panted as her release began to build inside her womb. "Oh god."

"Taste me," he whispered as his mouth covered hers again.

The taste of his blood as it filled her mouth was warm, spicy. He'd cut his own tongue on his fangs. She sucked at it, tentatively at first then hungrily as his warmth spread through her limbs. It was like being drugged and when he pulled his mouth away she whimpered, wanting it back again. Wanting more of his taste.

"Small steps, baby," he murmured, then ground his hips against her clit, sending sparks showering through her head.

She screamed as pleasure and pain mingled. Her body was changing, she could feel it as her orgasm raced through her, building with each thrust of his cock into her pussy until she exploded into a million pieces. Her body contorted under his as he thrust harder, ringing another even more powerful orgasm from her body.

Feelings were more intense, colors brighter as she crested, barely holding onto a conscious state as feelings of euphoria swam through her. With a growl Marcus tensed above her, spilling his seed into her channel. She could feel every burning drop as it released from his cock, every convulsion from her pussy as it squeezed his cock dry. She could feel it all— everything—and shuddered from head to toe.

God, she'd had no idea it could be like that.

"I love you," she whispered.

The last words she heard before drifting off into a deep state of sleep were, "I love you too, sweet. My beautiful sweet."

* * * * *

Sitting at the small table in the corner of the kitchen, Rebecca gazed out at the early morning darkness. It was still an hour yet before sunrise but she hadn't been able to sleep anymore. She needed to get up, get more of her strength back.

Darien had been reluctant but finally relented, making sure to stay close by her side the whole time.

She held out her arm, running her finger over the light pink line that slashed across her wrist. One more day and it would be completely gone. She was still amazed she'd survived it. Amazed she'd had the courage and strength to make the spell work.

"Good morning."

Rebecca glanced at Tonya from the corner of her eye as she bent and placed a quick kiss on her cheek.

"I'm glad to see you're up and about," Tonya said, a beautiful smile tugging at her lips.

"You're up awfully early," Rebecca said with a grin.

"Marcus and I spent most of the night talking and I suddenly had a craving for a huge breakfast."

Narrowing her eyes, Rebecca studied her closely. It wasn't just her smile that was beautiful. It was all of her. Her friend had always been pretty, but now... My god, now she was stunning.

"You did it, didn't you?" Rebecca gasped.

Tonya's smile widened as she nodded her head. Leaning forward, she placed her hands on the table in front of her. "Rebecca, it's amazing. I can't even describe it."

"Are you happy?"

"More than I've ever been. I promise."

Rebecca took a deep breath and nodded. "Then that's all that matters."

The grin that spread Tonya's lips could be described as nothing less than breathtaking. Marcus strolled into the breakfast room, their new meeting place since Darien wouldn't let Rebecca outside. He was terrified the demons would try to take her again and if she were honest so was she. Pursing her lips, she studied Marcus intently.

"Hurt her and I'll drive a stake through your heart."

His eyes widened for just a second and then his lips twitched in amusement.

"She means it too," Darien murmured as he walked past Marcus to take the seat next to her at the table. With a wink, he placed a coffee cup in front of her.

Marcus placed his hand over his heart, his face sobering into a mask of sincerity. "I promise you. She'll be fine."

Rebecca picked up her cup, bringing it to her lips and inhaling the strong scent of coffee. "She better be *better* than fine," Rebecca snarled.

With a wry grin, Marcus pulled out the chair next to Tonya and sat. "Should I drag the old metal armor from the basement? Sounds like I might need it."

Darien choked on his coffee and Rebecca hid her grin behind her cup. "Don't do anything wrong and you'll be fine."

"Don't mind her," Tonya began with a wave of her hand. "She's just pissy because she can't go outside."

"I hate being cooped up like this," Rebecca grumbled. "I want this over."

Darien put his hand over hers, giving it a gentle squeeze. "We all do."

"Nicholas still working on spells?" Marcus asked.

With a nod, Darien set his cup on the table. "Yes. When he and Vincent aren't arguing, that is."

"I'm not sure who I feel more sorry for," Rebecca said with a sideways grin, her mind imagining Nicholas and Vincent at each other's throats, "Nicholas or the cat."

A deep chuckle rumbled through Darien's chest, making Rebecca's insides simmer with desire. She still felt weak, tired, but she had no doubt she could find the energy to make love to her warlocks again.

"It's been like that since we were kids. Vincent was our tutor, teaching us about magic."

"When did you get involved with black magic?" Rebecca asked.

"Nicholas started delving into it when we were told about you. Several of the protection spells we've used are from black magic. Vincent, though most people don't know this, especially the council, is quite proficient in it."

"But isn't black magic off limits?"

"Mostly, yes. There are also some spells that are forbidden."

"Like the one Nicholas was going to use yesterday?" Tonya asked.

Rebecca frowned. "What was Nicholas going to do yesterday?"

Darien turned to her with a gaze that made her toes curl. "Come after you."

"He's broken through the barrier," Nicholas snarled as he and Vincent stormed into the small breakfast nook.

Rebecca's heart began to pound in fear. Real fear. "Who?"

Nicholas reached down to take her hand in his, tugging her up. "Sebastian."

A deep rumble filled the room, shaking the very walls around them. Turning, Rebecca watched in horror as the huge picture window behind the table shook then shattered, sending tiny shards of sharp glass raining down around her. She squealed, shielding her face from the debris. Darien wrapped his arms around her, shielding her as well.

"Tonya, upstairs," Marcus shouted over the noise.

Nicholas held up his hand, stopping her. "No. We stick together. He could get to her if she's alone."

"I won't have her in the middle of this, Nicholas."

"We don't have a choice," Darien snapped. "She's safer with you than alone. You know it."

Raising her gaze, Rebecca looked over at Tonya. She stood next to Marcus, more angry than afraid. She knew her friend. She would have never agreed to leave Marcus right now. Marcus moved Tonya behind him, shielding her from the man walking across the lawn.

Sebastian.

Rebecca's fingers gripped Darien's arm, her nails digging into his flesh as her anxiety grew to outright fear. This man was stronger than her, a lot stronger than her. She didn't stand a chance alone against him

"You're not alone," Nicholas whispered and some of her bravado returned.

As he stalked forward angrily the wind blew his cape, forcing it behind his body to flap in the breeze. His long white hair remained in place, his cold eyes piercing as they locked onto her with evil intent.

"*Tigala,*" Nicholas shouted and a soft blue glow shimmered across the open window before disappearing seconds later.

Sebastian came to a stop. Raising his hands, he shoved his palms toward the window. The shield Nicholas had erected changed to glass as it shattered. Grabbing her around the waist, Nicholas turned her, putting his back toward the window. She heard his grunt of pain as shards of glass pierced the flesh of his back. Twisting from his arms, Rebecca turned to stare in horror as he dropped to his knees, his back covered in blood.

"Nicholas," she screamed, rushing to his side.

Darien grabbed her, pulling her away from Nicholas and toward the den off the kitchen. "Vincent will take care of him."

As she watched, Vincent put his paw on Nicholas's back, his eyes closed as he recited a spell. Marcus and Tonya followed close behind as the four of them headed through the den and into the grand salon overlooking the backyard, Sebastian close on their heels.

"That was more than just glass that hit Nicholas, wasn't it?" Rebecca demanded.

"Yes." Darien nodded, glancing quickly around the room.

"We have to make a stand," Marcus growled.

"I agree."

"What about Nicholas?" Rebecca demanded.

Darien turned and gripped her shoulders, giving her a slight shake. "Nicholas will be fine, Becca. I promise. But right now you have to keep a level head. Concentrate. Because it's going to take all of us to fight him."

Swallowing her dread, she nodded. He was right. Nicholas had told her the most important element of any spell was concentration. She had to keep her head clear.

Chapter Twelve

ɞ

Rebecca watched Darien, fear gripping her heart as he turned to face Sebastian.

"*Leenana,*" Darien shouted and blew against his upturned palm.

A ball of red light flew from his hand straight toward Sebastian. With a nasty smile Sebastian raised his palm and with a flick of his wrist the ball changed direction, flying right toward Darien and hitting him square in the chest. He was thrust backward ten feet, landing against the wall with a grunt. He slid silently to the floor, his eyes closed.

"Darien!" she shouted and made a move to help him but Sebastian's dark growl made her stop short.

"Now for you, bitch."

Sebastian stalked toward her. The determination in his gaze sent a shiver of apprehension down her spine and she took a step back before stopping herself. She refused to be afraid—refused to let him win. Squaring her shoulders, she met his stare and prepared to defend herself against him.

Off to her left, Marcus growled. Sebastian halted and turned to stare at Marcus with an angry growl. Rebecca gasped as the two vampires squared off against one another. Marcus curled his lip, showing sharp distended fangs and blue eyes that seemed to glow iridescent in his anger.

"Marcus, don't," she whispered.

"Stay back, Rebecca."

"No," Sebastian taunted. "Let her come. Let her feel what it's like to have the blood sucked from her body."

With a growl, Marcus lunged. Sebastian rose up, meeting Marcus halfway across the room. They collided five feet off the floor. Locked together, they each struggled to gain the upper hand. Marcus gripped Sebastian by the neck and Sebastian gasped for air, his fingers clawing at Marcus' hand.

"Marcus!" Tonya screamed.

Vincent jumped onto the back of the chair, his angry blue gaze piercing Tonya. "Don't interfere, Tonya. Marcus can handle him."

Tonya looked ready to argue, ready to bolt forward and help. Nicholas staggered into the room behind them, obviously still weak, but the anger flashing in his gaze frightened even Rebecca.

Above them Sebastian struggled against Marcus. They moved toward Rebecca and she backed away, scrambling to check on Darien, who still remained motionless on the floor. A movement next to the French door caught her attention and she stared wide-eyed, her fingers trembling with uncertainty.

Marcus's father Jullian stood in the open French doorway, a crossbow raised and aimed directly at the two fighting vampires, his expression cold and unreadable. Should she scream? Warn them?

Which one was he aiming at?

Turning, she yelled, "Marcus, look out."

Jullian fired the crossbow. The short bolt flew through the air as if in slow motion, straight for Sebastian's back. Sebastian howled, his body going rigid as the the silver-tipped bolt sank into his flesh, exiting the other side and missing Marcus' shoulder by mere inches. Both Marcus and Sebastian dropped to the floor.

Tonya ran forward, grasping Marcus' elbow and helping him to stand. Sebastian curled on the floor in pain, staring blindly toward the ceiling, his whole body shaking uncontrollably.

"Jullian," Sebastian gasped.

Marcus looked up and stared at Jullian, shock draining the color from his face. "Did you mean to hit him or me?" Marcus snarled.

Jullian snorted. "Don't be ridiculous. Him. Unfortunately my aim wasn't perfect." He threw the crossbow to the floor, his lip snarling. "It's been a long time since I've had to use one of those."

"He's suffering," Tonya murmured as she stared in disgust at Sebastian.

Marcus shook his head. "Let him."

Darien groaned and Rebecca turned to help him stand. He wobbled slightly as he came to his feet and she gripped his elbow, helping him to keep his balance. His eyes widened slightly as they landed on a bloody Sebastian and then Jullian.

"Damn," Darien mumbled, raising his hand to touch the back of his head. "It seems I missed all the fun."

Rebecca moved to stand over Sebastian. His normally cold blue eyes now stared at her pleadingly, the color now almost as white as his skin. "He's still alive," she mumbled.

"Get away from him, Rebecca," Nicholas shouted and she raised her hand, stopping him from coming any closer.

To her surprise he stopped, staring at her with a mixture of concern and curiosity. "You killed my parents," she snarled.

Sebastian swallowed and nodded his head. "And I would do it again," he croaked.

Anger seethed through Rebecca, almost choking her. He'd taken everything away from her. Her family, her heritage. Everything. Grasping one of his hands, she tugged, pulling him toward the door that would lead them to the backyard. Red tinged the horizon, indicating the sun wouldn't be far behind. It was time this warlock-vampire met his end.

"Rebecca, what are you doing?" Nicholas shouted.

She turned to look at him as he leaned heavily against the doorframe. Whatever the stuff had been that had pierced him had drained him, left him weak. "Just stay there. This is for me to do."

"Rebecca, no!" Sebastian screamed, fighting against her hold.

Turning, Rebecca snapped, "*Vilat.*" Sebastian froze, starring up at her with wide, frightened eyes.

With a huff, she continued to pull him across the veranda and down into the yard. The horizon was brighter now, the sun not far behind.

Marcus stood back, staring at his father in shock. Jullian had actually saved his life. "How did you know?"

"I've been following him for a couple of days now. I knew he was up to something, just wasn't sure what."

Nodding, Marcus wrapped his arm around Tonya's waist, holding her tightly to him. Jullian's lips lifted in a sad smile as he studied them. "It's good that she loved you enough," Jullian replied softly.

Marcus knew what he meant and gave Tonya a slight squeeze. "She loved you, Jullian. She regretted her decision."

Jullian inclined his head slightly to the side. "She told you this?"

"Yes. Just before she died. She missed you," he added softly.

Sadness filled Jullian's eyes but he tried to hide it by turning away from them. "The sun's coming up. I have to go." Jullian's gaze met his and for the first time in his life Marcus felt as though his father accepted him. Loved him. He could see it in his eyes, even though he knew his father would probably never be able to say it.

"You remind me so much of your mother." Jullian smiled slightly. "I've never been ashamed of you, Marcus. You are my son and I'm proud of you."

Marcus's eyes widened in shock. *Guess I was wrong.*

With a nod to Tonya, Jullian disappeared in a cloud of gray smoke. Tonya gasped then turned to Marcus with a cheeky grin. "Can you do that?"

He smiled slightly. "No. *We* cannot. We're not full-blooded. But I can cast a spell that would do the same thing."

Darien moved forward to lean against a wingback chair, his gaze narrowing on Rebecca as she continued to drag Sebastian across the yard. "What the hell is she doing?"

"Sunlight," Marcus replied, nodding toward the horizon.

"Shit," Nicholas cried, then took off out of the house, close on Rebecca's heels.

Rebecca grunted, pulling Sebastian to a small clearing a few feet from the veranda. "Rebecca," she heard Nicholas warn.

Turning, she saw him and Darien running toward her. "This will work, right?" she asked.

"Move away from him, Becca," Darien warned. "You're too close."

The spell wore off and Sebastian screamed as sunlight broke over the horizon and slashed across his body. She covered her ears, blocking out the horrendous sound of his pain as his body contorted at her feet.

"Rebecca, move!" Nicholas shouted but she barely heard him over Sebastian's screaming.

She glanced questioningly at Nicholas who raised his hand and shouted something she couldn't hear. A force hit her square in the chest, knocking her backward onto the damp ground and stealing the very breath from her lungs. She gasped, rolling to her knees and trying to catch her breath. Sebastian's screams still echoed around her and she cringed, turning to stare at the smoking body just a few feet away.

Without warning he combusted, exploding as his body erupted into intense red flames. Rebecca squealed, moving back even farther to get away from the searing heat licking at her flesh. No wonder Nicholas had knocked her back. If she hadn't moved she'd have burned right along with him.

Nicholas and Darien both grasped her hands, tugging her to her feet and away from the burning body. The smell of ash and burning flesh filled the air, making her gag. She turned away, unable to take any more of the images.

"It's okay. It's over," Nicholas whispered as he wrapped his arms around her and held her tight.

Darien rubbed her arms, bringing warmth to her chilled skin. Burying her face in Nicholas' chest, she finally let her bravado fall and burst into hard, racking sobs that shook her whole body.

Epilogue
Two weeks later.

ဆ

Rebecca glanced around the massive ballroom in awe. The pictures Darien and Nicholas had shown her before didn't do the event justice. Candlelight flickered from candelabras and side tables. Fountains overflowing with champagne graced the numerous tables throughout the room along with finger foods and flowers of every color imaginable.

An older couple nodded in their direction and she tensed. Nicholas had pointed the woman out earlier. She was Margaret Van Marshe, lead council woman. She was the one Nicholas and Darien had spent three hours explaining things to yesterday.

"Relax," Darien whispered in her ear, his voice carrying a slight flicker of amusement. "You look beautiful."

How I look isn't the problem, she answered in her mind.

Darien smiled slightly with a nod, indicating he'd heard her. She'd finally learned how to communicate with them through her thoughts. The whole idea had been very unsettling, at least at first but she'd gotten used to it and better at it.

Nicholas placed a hand at the small of her back for support, which she was hugely grateful for. Tonya and Marcus stood to the side, Vincent at their feet, his tail swishing as though he didn't have a care in the world.

Margaret and her companion strolled over slowly then came to a stop directly in front of her. Rebecca bowed her head slightly in greeting. Margaret nodded in return, her regal stance quite dominating, making Rebecca all the more nervous.

A small smile tugged at the older woman's lips, putting a sparkle in her observant gray eyes. "God, you look so much like your mother. But I think I see a little of your father in you also." Turning to her companion, she asked, "Don't you think, François?"

François nodded, his green eyes studying Rebecca's face closely. "Yes, Madam Chancellor."

"You've had a rough couple of weeks, Rebecca. How are you holding up?"

"As well as can be expected, I suppose."

"Good. I'll expect you to keep these two in line." She used her closed fan to point toward Nicholas and Darien.

Rebecca nodded. "Yes, Madam," she murmured.

Margaret's lips spread into a wide smile. "Margaret, dear. You're a member of the council now. Vincent will tutor you on rules and what not so you're ready for the next meeting." She turned to look down on the cat at her feet. "Won't you, Vincent?"

Vincent meowed in response.

"Mada…Margaret," Rebecca began, wringing her hands in front of her.

"Yes, dear?"

Rebecca licked her lips and almost faltered at the older woman's knowing gaze. "Wouldn't it be easier for Vincent to tutor me if he were human?" Vincent rose to all fours, his wide gaze watching Margaret closely. "After all, he did help me with Sebastian."

"I'm well aware of what he did," Margaret began with a nod. "And under the circumstances I believe you're right. It would be easier."

With a wave of her hand, Vincent morphed from a cat to one very gorgeous male. He stood tall, close to six-foot-three, and had wide shoulders that tapered down to a flat stomach and thick thighs. Long ebony hair similar to Nicholas' and

Darien's cascaded down his back to a trim waist and hips. A black tuxedo flattered his figure and deep, almost navy blue eyes.

Damn.

"Finally," he sighed and his hands patted his chest then further down to his thighs, making Rebecca giggle. "I thought I was going to be a cat forever."

He turned to Rebecca and smiled, making him appear even more handsome.

"Behave yourself," Margaret replied in a firm voice. "Or you will be again."

Vincent bowed toward Margaret. "I promise you, my lady. I will be on my very best behavior."

"Sure you will," Margaret drawled and Rebecca bit back a knowing laugh.

If Vincent was the same in human form as he had been as a cat the world was in for one hell of a ride.

"Nicholas." Vincent turned and smiled brightly toward Nicholas. "Where are the car keys?"

Rebecca laughed. True to his word, Vincent wanted to drive a car. "On the dresser," she whispered and Vincent disappeared in a flash.

Nicholas frowned. "You realize he's never driven a car before. And how did you know my keys were on my dresser?"

She smiled wickedly, making Margaret laugh as well. "Oh, she's going to be quite the challenge for you two.

Darien came up behind her and placed his hands on her shoulders, giving them a gentle squeeze that made her stomach flutter. "I don't know about Nicholas. But it's a challenge I'm looking forward to."

"So am I," Nicholas whispered before placing a soft kiss on her temple.

If the truth were known, so was she. She'd never been happier in her life.

Tonya smiled, watching the three of them. She'd never seen Rebecca happier and the twins were good for her. Over her friend's shoulder she noticed Jullian. He stood off to the side, his gaze taking in the scene from a distance. His tux hugged his wide shoulders and lean hips, the white of the shirt and vest complementing his ebony hair. He and Marcus looked so much alike. More like brothers than father and son.

"I'll be right back," she murmured to Marcus.

"Where are you going?"

"To get some champagne. You stay here with them." She nodded to Nicholas and Darien who still stood talking with Margaret.

Instead of heading straight toward Jullian she moved to the right and the champagne fountain on the far side of the room, hoping Jullian would follow. Lifting a small champagne flute, she held the crystal beneath the fountain, filling her glass.

"He's lucky to have you." Jullian spoke softly, his voice close to her ear.

"He would be lucky to have you as well."

Turning, she met his hypnotic gaze head-on. As a full-blooded vampire Jullian was stunning. But coldness surrounded him like a shroud. This was a man who didn't let anybody get too close.

"He has me," Jullian murmured. "When he needs me."

Glancing over Jullian's shoulder, she caught sight of Marcus as he came to stand just behind his father.

"Why don't the two of you try again?" she asked, watching sadness cloud over Jullian's intense eyes.

"Marcus doesn't need a father. He grew up just fine."

"That's not true. Every man needs a father."

The corner of his lips lifted in a sad smile. Behind him Marcus frowned. "Marcus and I are from two different worlds. He's my son and I will always love him but our worlds don't

171

mesh. I detest magic and he detests my world. I appreciate what you're trying to do but this way is for the best."

Tonya shook her head in denial and Jullian pressed a finger to her lips, silencing what she was about to say. "Love him," he whispered then smiled slightly. "Good night, Marcus," he added before winking at Tonya.

She stared in surprise. He'd known all along Marcus was behind him? In shock she watched him walk away.

"Jullian," Marcus called.

Jullian stopped and turned to look at his son. She could see the sadness in his gaze, the loneliness that ate him up inside. It made her heart ache just to look at him.

He shook his head then gave them a nod before disappearing in a cloud of smoke. Marcus sighed and Tonya moved to wrap her arm around his elbow. "He'll come around in time," she sighed.

Marcus placed his hand over hers and she admired how his strong fingers looked as they caressed hers against the sleeve of his tuxedo.

"It's been over three hundred years. How much time do you think he needs?"

"As much as it takes," she whispered. "He's still hurting, Marcus. He must have loved her so much."

With a sigh, he leaned down and placed a kiss on the top of her head. "I don't want you to ever regret what you did," he murmured.

"I won't." She turned and stared up at him, letting all the love she felt for him show in her gaze. "I love you."

His lips spread into a beautiful smile that stole her breath. "I love you."

"Save it for later," Nicholas drawled, taking her attention away from Marcus.

"Kiss my ass, warlock," Marcus snarled.

Rebecca chuckled then moved to pry her friend away from the handsome vampire. "Was that Jullian you were talking to?" she asked.

Tonya nodded. "I'll tell you all about it later."

"So have you told Tonya yet?" Darien teased and Rebecca didn't miss the slight widening of her friend's gaze.

"Told me what?" Tonya asked.

Marcus shrugged. "Well I thought since Rebecca would be busy with her training that you and I would take a little trip."

"A trip where?" Tonya asked with growing excitement.

"France."

"France?" Rebecca and Tonya both cried in unison.

"I have a house there."

"A château," Nicholas corrected. "And it's attached to one of the largest vineyards in France."

Tonya's gaze widened and Marcus grinned, his shoulder lifting in a slight shrug. "What can I say? We're wealthy."

"And you couldn't have told me this?" Tonya gasped.

"Does it matter?" Marcus asked.

"Well…"

Rebecca nudged her in the side. "You know damn good and well it doesn't so don't even go there."

Tonya winked at her. Turning to Marcus, she eyed him speculatively. "I suppose I forgive you."

Marcus snorted but his lips twitched in amusement. "Damn women. No wonder Jullian avoids relationships like the plague."

"That's enough, *children*," Nicholas drawled. "Get along. We have a double wedding to get ready for."

"Double wedding?" Rebecca glanced toward her twins who stared at her with adorable smiles.

"I know you said you wouldn't marry us," Darien began as he slowly walked toward her. "But we were hoping you'd changed your mind, Madam Councilwoman."

Her gaze moved from Darien to Nicholas, who watched her closely, his gaze expectant. She ignored the title. She couldn't get past what they were saying. Her heart pounded in her chest with excitement. Marry them?

"How can I marry both of you? That's not even legal."

"You'll legally marry Nicholas," Darien said with a nod toward his brother. "But privately marry me."

"I see. So are you asking?" she pried.

"Yes," they replied in unison and she smiled, nodding her head.

"Yes," she said with a giggle. "Of course the answer is yes."

Laughing, she threw herself into their open arms.

Also by Trista Ann Michaels

ဆ

Callie's Sexy Surprise

Crossing the Line

Fantasy Bar

Fantasy Resort

Holiday Love Lessons

Star Crossed

About the Author

৪৩

Trista penned her first ghost story at the age of eight. She still has a love of ghosts, but her taste and writing style have leaned more to the sultry side. She started writing erotic romance two years ago, and with the help of her critique partners was soon published. She's been running full steam ever since.

Raised an Air Force brat, Trista surprised her family by marrying a Navy man. But just as she knew he would, her husband won them over despite his military choice. Together they've had three children, and she attributes their successful marriage to the fact he's away flying a lot. Separation does make the heart grow fonder. After all, if he's not here, she can't kill him.

All joking aside, her family and writing partners are her biggest form of support and encouragement. Trista's a big believer in happily ever after and although she may put her characters through hell getting there, they will always achieve that goal.

Trista welcomes comments from readers. You can find her website and email address on her author bio page at www.ellorascave.com.

Tell Us What You Think

We appreciate hearing reader opinions about our books. You can email us at Comments@EllorasCave.com.

Why an electronic book?

We live in the Information Age—an exciting time in the history of human civilization, in which technology rules supreme and continues to progress in leaps and bounds every minute of every day. For a multitude of reasons, more and more avid literary fans are opting to purchase e-books instead of paper books. The question from those not yet initiated into the world of electronic reading is simply: *Why?*

1. *Price.* An electronic title at Ellora's Cave Publishing and Cerridwen Press runs anywhere from 40% to 75% less than the cover price of the exact same title in paperback format. Why? Basic mathematics and cost. It is less expensive to publish an e-book (no paper and printing, no warehousing and shipping) than it is to publish a paperback, so the savings are passed along to the consumer.

2. *Space.* Running out of room in your house for your books? That is one worry you will never have with electronic books. For a low one-time cost, you can purchase a handheld device specifically designed for e-reading. Many e-readers have large, convenient screens for viewing. Better yet, hundreds of titles can be stored within your new library—on a single microchip. There are a variety of e-readers from different manufacturers. You can also read e-books on your PC or laptop computer. (Please note that Ellora's Cave does not endorse any specific brands.

You can check our websites at www.ellorascave.com or www.cerridwenpress.com for information we make available to new consumers.)

3. **_Mobility._**   Because your new e-library consists of only a microchip within a small, easily transportable e-reader, your entire cache of books can be taken with you wherever you go.

4. **_Personal Viewing Preferences._**   Are the words you are currently reading too small? Too large? Too… ANNOYING? Paperback books cannot be modified according to personal preferences, but e-books can.

5. **_Instant Gratification._**   Is it the middle of the night and all the bookstores near you are closed? Are you tired of waiting days, sometimes weeks, for bookstores to ship the novels you bought? Ellora's Cave Publishing sells instantaneous downloads twenty-four hours a day, seven days a week, every day of the year. Our webstore is never closed. Our e-book delivery system is 100% automated, meaning your order is filled as soon as you pay for it.

Those are a few of the top reasons why electronic books are replacing paperbacks for many avid readers.

As always, Ellora's Cave and Cerridwen Press welcome your questions and comments. We invite you to email us at Comments@ellorascave.com or write to us directly at Ellora's Cave Publishing Inc., 1056 Home Avenue, Akron, OH 44310-3502.

Discover for yourself why readers can't get enough of the multiple award-winning publisher Ellora's Cave.

Whether you prefer e-books or paperbacks,

be sure to visit EC on the web at www.ellorascave.com

for an erotic reading experience that will leave you breathless.

Printed in Great Britain by
Amazon.co.uk, Ltd.,
Marston Gate.